Knuckleheads

KNUCKLE-HEADS

stories

Jeff Kass

1334 Woodbourne Street
Westland, MI 48186
www.dzancbooks.org

Published 2011 by Dzanc Books
Book design by Steven Seighman

Some of these stories have appeared in various forms in *Current,
Bull Men's Fiction, Unsquared: Ann Arbor Writers Unleash Their Edgiest
Poems & Stories*, and *Writecorner*.

06 07 08 09 10 11 5 4 3 2
First edition March 2011
ISBN-13: 978-0982797518

Printed in the United States of America

*The characters and events in this book are fictitious. Any similarity to real persons,
living or dead, is coincidental and not intended by the author.*

CONTENTS

For Karen, patient host of long-time knucklehead-in-residence.

DON'T MESS

Nobody had ever imagined cheerleaders for a wrestling team before.

Certainly, nobody had imagined cute cheerleaders for a wrestling team, girls with hair styled neatly, side-wept, sweet-smelling. Girls who floated through the stench and chill of the gym like an alien fog, mystics in saddle-shoes. Confused, my teammates and I watched them, and smelled them, and were stunned by them. Nobody understood how to act because, yeah, we knew about girls – sort of – but girls who would surrender an entire Saturday, from 8am to 11pm, to clap their hands and stomp their feet at a *wrestling tournament?*

Nobody had ever heard of something like that.

None of our coaches had heard of mouth-guards either, though now it seems obvious. They should have known where to get a kid some molded plastic to protect his lips and gums from the braces girding his teeth. Seems like they could have suggested a sporting goods store, or ordered something from a catalogue, but they never did.

They did know about top seeds, how to pluck spindly anonymous boys from the high school hallways and sculpt them into thick-muscled names Magic-Markered onto the first line of tournament brackets. Three hours of daily grueling practice. The moment we slouched, their whistles screeched in our ears, shrill and continuous, like the high-pitched cries of colicky babies. From whistle to whistle we feinted and spun and pushed and grabbed, our coaches sure we learned the holds that hurt. They worked their knotted forearms into the backs of our necks so we'd understand the pain we were capable of instilling. They knew how to fight for those top seeds too. How to speak up in pre-tourney meetings, grim and certain – "My guy's gonna roll through this weight-class," they'd say. "Trust me, he's tough."

So I was. Tough. Able to snap back the head of a kid who stole from my locker the forty dollars I'd saved to buy a birthday present for a girl I wanted to like, and to bounce his skull off an aluminum doorframe. Tough enough to stare down a different kid in a parking-garage with a tire-iron gripped in his palm, saying only, "That's not a good choice for you now, *is it?*"

Tough enough too to be named top seed at 138 lbs. in the Peru Tournament in Plattsburgh, a cold farmtown with a locker room so cold we could see our breath when we stripped to our boxers and weighed in on an enormous cattle scale. We were a handful of miles from the Canadian border and we were freezing. We wanted to hurt people and get back on the bus and get the fuck home.

I took that responsibility seriously. With two quick pins engraved on the bracket chart, I did my job with efficiency, easily reaching the semifinals against the fourth seed. He looked tough too. Shoulders thick like turkeys. More unshaven stubble on his face than I'd be able to grow for another decade. One of the cute cheerleaders, maybe the cutest cheerleader, stroked that stubble as she tongue-kissed him minutes before our match; her fingers crawling across his cheeks, her legs somehow tan in the middle of winter, her dark hair thick and curly, like a soft cloud on her back.

That was some bullshit.

You don't make out with your girlfriend, no matter how cute, when you're seeded fourth and you're about to face the top-ranked wrestler in your weight-class. Not when he can see you making out and he's warming up in that arctic drafty gym, bouncing from one foot to the other, shaking his arms loose, seething. Because what he's thinking is that you don't respect him. He's the top seed and you're treating him like he's some guppy you're going to flop onto his back. What he's thinking is he'd like nothing better than not only to beat you, but to humiliate you in front of your hot cheerleader girlfriend. He wants you on your back, his breath thick on your neck, you squirming, hoping you're still going to get some – maybe – after your girl sees you weak, pathetic, beaten.

It's difficult to measure rage.

There's no scale that plots your x and y coordinates at 7.7 pissed off when your dad grounds you for wearing your basketball sneakers in the snowstorm and you miss the party where Cara – the saucy girl who sold them to you at the Footlocker – said she'd meet you; 8.2 pissed off when you fail your first driving test after parallel-parking your rear bumper into a fire hydrant; 9.5 the Monday after the party when you see Cara in the hallway holding hands with your teammate.

When that whistle blew, I flew at the fourth seed like a rabid raccoon. Sucked his leg to my chest as if I were prepared to eat it for dinner, tripped his other leg and plummeted him onto his back. Maybe I bashed my face into his knee. I don't know what I felt. My mouth stung and there was ripped skin and blood and I swallowed some but I kept surging. Straight through him. The whole thing could have been over in thirty seconds, but that would have been too easy. He could have told his girlfriend it was just one move, I got lucky. Fuck luck. Luck was not part of this equation. I punished the kid on his back, let him squirm and breathe my hot stink, then let him scramble to his knees so he could think maybe he had a chance.

There's no way I could have distinguished any specific voices in the roar of that moment, but I like to imagine I did hear one – the cheerleader with the dark curls yelling, "C'mon Sweetheart! You can do it!" All the while I'm thinking, No, Sweetheart, you can't, and I'm grinding my forearm into the back of his head, trying to crush his face into the floor so he's inhaling sweat and shoe-bottom dirt, and there are easier ways to turn some arrogant fish with turkey shoulders onto his back, quicker ways, but this situation called only for the most painful way – the double arm-bar.

Imagine you're lying face-down in the street and some roid-ripped police officer's got his knee jammed between your shoulder-blades. Then he takes his nightstick and hooks it beneath one of your arms so it's nestled inside the crook of your elbow, then he pulls backward so it feels like your rotator cuff is being yanked through your skin. While you're dealing with that blast of pain, he proceeds to thread the other end of the nightstick under your other arm, so he can wrench both your shoulders from their sockets.

Imagine he twists the nightstick.

Imagine he walks out to the side of your body so his entire weight leverages your torso, spinning your neck and head, until you're driven onto your back, both your arms knotted beneath you, your shoulders digging into concrete.

That's the double arm-bar, and the kid deserved it.

His half-swallowed yelps only made me lock his arms up more tightly, only made me spike my chin into his upper back and extend myself so the maximum amount of pressure could be applied to his shoulders and neck. Then, too fast – putting someone away with an arm-bar was not only painful, but slow – I heard the slap of palm on mat. Except, it wasn't the referee's palm, it was *his* palm – the stubble-faced kid – signaling he wanted the match stopped because he was injured.

More bullshit.

I'd hurt him, sure, he deserved to be hurt, but no bones had snapped. No ligaments had popped. He wasn't injured. He was faking, pretending he was damaged so he could spare himself the indignity of being pinned; so he could confess to his girlfriend that his shoulder had been hurt before the match. He went in hobbled and tried valiantly to soldier through. That's why he lost.

I tried to stay loose, sloshing the spit and blood around in my mouth, tasting it, bouncing from foot to foot, shaking my arms as the referee waited the requisite two minutes to see if the so-called injured wrestler could continue. I felt a hot orange wave, then a black one, scraping like a cheese-grater across my forehead, tightening the muscles in my thighs. I pushed down hard with my feet, tried to shove them through the floor. People were shouting at wrestlers in other matches, urging them to break free from a hold or to lift somebody in the air and slam him. I couldn't do anything. I ran in place.

That turkey-shouldered kid knew the code. Had to know it. He was fourth seed, out of sixteen. You don't get there without rolling a bunch of kids on their necks. He knew where the line of truly injuring someone was, and he also knew we hadn't crossed it. I shook my arms, licked the bands on my teeth, waited.

The thing about strength is that it's gritty.

I first understood I was strong in third grade. On a steel-grey day when Daniel Meyers cut in front of Susie London in the four-square line. That was against the code too, cutting the four-square line, sneaking in when a horde of other kids had been waiting patiently for the chance to star on the asphalt stage, to batter the ball from one chalked box to another until someone missed. There was a rhythm to that anticipation – the running from the lunchroom to claim a spot toward the front of the line, the waiting as the ball bounced from square to square searching out which kid to send hangdog to the rear.

It was wrong to mess with that rhythm, wrong to cut into the line as if your hands battering the ball were more important than anyone else's.

I don't remember moving, but I remember what happened when my hand gripped the hood of Daniel's sweatshirt and pulled. He careened backward and smashed into the school's brick wall. The four-square line, quiet, watched Daniel stumble to his feet and rub the back of his head, then lick the blood from his fingers where he'd scraped his knuckles. I wasn't surprised I'd tossed him like that, that he'd flown into the wall, only that it had been the slight against Susie London that had provoked my wrath. What was it about this shy girl that had sparked this quick stretch of hand to sweatshirt hood, this ferocious grip and pull?

Susie seemed thrilled too, excited that a boy would send someone sprawling on her behalf, and became less shy around me, even agreed to wear my velour sweat-jacket during lunch hours, to let it swallow her when she was cold.

By junior high, Susie London had grown less shy around a lot of people and, to stay warm, wrapped herself in the St. Bernard's football jacket of a brutish kid named Christian Morris. At thirteen, he had a hedge of hair above his top lip and a square and sizable head, like a small microwave oven. On the day report cards came out, with my piss-poor behavioral grade in Mechanical Drawing sure to provoke a month-long grounding, I funneled all my bitterness into an arrow of sound – *You'd better stay away from Susie London* – and challenged Christian to a fight.

He sort of half-sung, the words pushing out rounder than I'd expected from his square head, *come on then*, and we trooped out of the cafeteria and down the stairs to the blacktop, a river of raucous classmates cheering behind. They hooted around Christian and me as we circled each other, wondering who would charge first. In the midst of one shuffle-step, I caught Susie's eye. She didn't look thrilled, or even scared, more like she was annoyed she'd been interrupted from finishing the half-eaten brownie wrapped in cellophane she held between her hands like a prayer-book.

You don't want me to do this? I stage-whispered, like a moron, as if anyone would. She nodded her head, which I took to mean she was answering, yes, I agree, I don't want you to do this, I just want to finish my brownie. Briefly, I considered taking the advice of the After-School Special preachers and walking away, but then Christian made the decision to rush me, to initiate a clumsy tackle by winding his arms around my legs. I shoved him away easily, my hands sliding aside the flat top of his head as if closing the drawer of a file cabinet.

Somehow, I was still thinking all this didn't have to happen. Maybe I could pick Christian up, shake his hand, tell him, *sorry, you don't actually have to stay away from Susie London. I was kidding. I have a bad grade in Mechanical Drawing. My parents are going to ground me. She's all yours.*

I may have even half-extended my hand to help Christian from the ground, but he grabbed it, tried to twist my arm – what did they teach these football players – and at that point there was no stopping. The momentum of the fight had claimed us: me, Christian, our cheering fans, even Susie. Christian's grip on my arm was weak, his hands sweaty, and even though he probably outweighed me by forty pounds, I knew I could repeat the toss of Daniel Meyers and flip Christian face-first into the brick wall a half-dozen feet behind us, his nose splattering blood like a perfect strike into the middle of the painted rectangle we used to play stickball.

But Susie's half-ambiguous nod had sucked the venom out of my desire to hurt Christian. What was the point of fighting if she didn't want me to? Christian wasn't a bad kid. Chunky, hairy, a bit slow, but we'd once killed an hour throwing rocks at a stop sign as we waited for our mothers to pick us up after detention. We hadn't spoken much, but we'd established a measure of comradeship, our rocks arcing toward the stop sign, occasionally bouncing off it with a metallic clang.

Now all I wanted was for the fight to be over, for everyone to go away and forget about it, for Susie not to hate me, for Christian not to break a cheekbone or a clavicle bumping into something. I let him headlock me. For whatever reason, he seemed happy to hold me there and halfheartedly aim a few punches at my ears, all of them missing. We stayed like that for maybe a minute, the crowd growing bored as he gripped my head and sort of punched while I wondered when an assistant principal would show up so Susie could at last unwrap her brownie.

When one did show up, he marched Christian and me down to the office, where I promptly advised him to send Christian back to the cafeteria. It was my fault. I'd challenged Christian to the fight. He'd just been stupid enough to accept. The principal, flummoxed by my willingness to absorb the entirety of the blame, let both of us go, adding only that he intended to talk to the wrestling coach about recruiting us for the coming season.

Back in the lunchroom, I tried to make it up with Susie by buying her another brownie. She seemed touched by the gift and broke up with Christian that evening over the phone. We dated for a week-and-a-half, after which she began to wear Michael Slauson's hockey jacket. Christian and I went out for wrestling. He quit in high school to work on cars and spend more time with Susie's younger sister Hannah, who had larger breasts. I got braces on my teeth in tenth grade to correct a slight overbite, didn't smile or kiss anybody for two years, and became a top seed.

There are few more blissful states than the moments immediately following winning a wrestling match. Having proven yourself stronger than some other kid who weighs the exact same you do, there's nothing left but to kick back – your muscles bulging in triumph – and spread yourself out in the bleachers as if you own them, while you imagine how shitty your opponent feels as he hurriedly pulls his sweats on in order to hide his naked loser skin. Winning in the semifinal round of a tournament is even better. If you win in the semis, you can lounge in the bleachers for the whole afternoon, even nap in them while just about everyone else in your weight-class beats each other up with the hopes of, at best, earning third place. You are not part of that consolation quagmire. You're going to the finals. Your name will be announced later, at night, after the whole gym has been cleared, and the National Anthem has been played, and people have paid additional admission to watch the house-lights dim and a spotlight shine while you latch up your headgear and battle for the title. After you've sufficiently owned the bleachers for a while, you can head into the locker room, shower and change into street clothes just so everyone in the gym knows you're in the finals. It's like you get to wear a sign that says, *I'm the nastiest badass at my weight in this whole damn building,* but it's just your clothes, just your beat-up blue jeans and sweatshirt, your work boots, so you're not even being obnoxious about it, just practical. Just everyday comfortable because that's who you are, everyday badass.

Stubble-face fuckboy with his fake injury ruined the whole deal. The referee blew his whistle to signal the injury time was over and then bent to ask the kid if he could continue. Punk shook his head as if there were truly nothing more tragic than the way his body had refused to allow itself to be tortured for an additional four-and-a-half minutes. When the ref raised my hand in victory and stubble-face leaned into his coach as he limped off the mat, as if he couldn't carry his own weight, as if the double arm-bar had somehow wrecked not only his arms, but also his legs, I gnashed my teeth. Hard.

Not only did the injury disqualification knock the kid out of the tournament, meaning he wouldn't have to wrestle all afternoon, but there was his adorable girlfriend wrapping an Ace bandage around an ice-pack on his shoulder and, with her other golden hand, tenderly rubbing his knee.

It was a ghastly sight. Horrid. Unjust. Yet, part of me remained hopeful. What if she was just feeling bad for him? I'd just destroyed her boyfriend, clearly illustrating what a dishrag he was, so maybe she was just taping his shoulder and rubbing his knee out of obligation. Maybe, as she helped him limp off to the locker room, she was going to whisper to me as she passed, *meet me in five minutes in the parking lot.* Maybe she was tired of her pathetic farmboy and intrigued by my downstate close-to-the-city mystery. Maybe we were going to brave the swirling winds and heat the tundra with our own tongue-kissing, her fingers crawling across my cheeks. Maybe my teammates on the bus would see it too, cleaning the fog from their windows with their forearms so they could see it better, and I'd be able to brag that I'd gotten her phone number.

It almost happened like that. As she helped her boyfriend fake-limp off, she turned, angling her thick brown eyes and sweet mouth to me and hissed, "You're mean. You're a mean person. Cocksucker."

Yeah, so.

I was mean.

That's what made me top seed. Some girls had to dig that. The dark-haired girl wasn't the only cheerleader who'd been there to root on the turkey kid. She'd just been the only one kissing him.

In fact, three other girls were approaching me, smiling, a giggling gaggle slithering toward the area of bleachers now under my legal jurisdiction. They weren't as cute as the one who'd called me a cocksucker, but they weren't nothing. They were girls in cheerleader skirts with long clean hair and chewing gum and legs and breasts. One of them stuck out her hand as if to shake mine and said, "Hi."

For the first time in two years, I smiled. Maybe all three of them would meet me in the parking lot. Maybe I'd have a trio of phone numbers to brag about. I opened my mouth to talk, to charm them with my wit, but then all that blood from where my braces had butchered the inside of my lips streamed down my chin and dripped onto my arms. The girl with her hand stuck out pulled it back in and grabbed the wrists of her friends. They ran from the bleachers as if I were some vampire, some horrible ghoul.

I was. I was some ghoul.

Some ghoul going to the finals.

My coach handed me a towel, and a lime-flavored sports drink in a squeeze-bottle. I swirled it in my mouth, mixed it with my spit, my metal, my blood. Everything that was left.

Guzzled.

PARENT-TEACHER CONFERENCE

Anthony Bassoli's put on close to a hundred pounds.

Twenty years ago, when we were in high school, he was a big kid, maybe six foot, one-eighty, a little puffy already. Now he's a blimp. The bottom part of his chin is rubbery and thick, an overcooked meatball falling farther with each moment he ages.

I can hear him wheeze as he walks toward me, a slow offbeat lumber, and there's nothing in his eyes that says he knows who I am. That's good, I guess, if a little insulting. We're the same age, but he could be fifteen years older. I've stayed in shape. He hasn't. Not even close.

He went to St. Regis High School, where I teach his son Ronald now. I was at Eastchester Central, and they used to beat us in baseball like we'd gotten drunk and crashed the family car and they were the furious father waiting with a strap. Our senior year E.C. had the best team I'd ever been on – finished second in our league – and there could have been an intense rivalry if we were even half as good as St. Regis, but we weren't. Anthony was just the third best pitcher on their squad – the Hunter brothers were both better – but he made us look like Little Leaguers. He only had one pitch, a fastball, but it was heat, and he could control it. He'd lace it on the corners, up and in or down and out, and send us muttering back to the bench as if our girlfriends had cheated the night before, inviting his steak-slab hands to paw their shirts in his Camaro. I could hit him because I ate fastballs, especially when I knew they were coming, but no one else on E.C. could.

When he faced us late in the season, they whacked us up and down the field. With our team down fourteen-zip, I stepped to the plate in the last inning pissed off, determined to rope another of Bassoli's heaters, to hit it hard somewhere and walk away with a perfect four-for-four day. To that point, I'd had our team's only three hits. I'd been vocal too, all game long trying to live up to my captain status and rally the troops. From my perch in leftfield, I'd machine-gunned a continuous barrage of *heywhaddayasaynows* and *nosticknows* and prior to leading off that last inning, I'd told my teammates – "Hey, we still have a chance. We can make history. I'll get on base and you keep it going. One little bingle at a time. Fourteen runs to tie, fifteen to win. Let's do it."

Bastard smirked at me when I dug into the box. Smirked. Then he shook his All-State catcher off about five times. Shithead only had one pitch. Finally, he nodded, smirked some more. Practically giggled. Then the ball flew like a missile dead at my skull. No way I could duck it, and it cracked my helmet like a hard left hook. Bleary-eyed, I crashed to the dirt. The field was spinning and loud and quiet at the same time, but I clawed back to my feet because fuck them with their fourteen-nothing lead, and the bastard was still smirking, staring me down like, Yup, I threw at you, now what?

What was me stalking toward him, not really sure what I was going to do when I got there but fuck him and his smirk and his team always winning, when All-State Catcher jumped on my back and tried to lock his arm around my neck.

Clearly All-State Catcher did not know I was All-State Wrestler. All it took was two hands to his wrist, a quick weight-shift of my hips, a shrug forward of shoulders, and he was flat and befuddled on the ground.

My teammates flocked from the bench, half of them wrestlers too. After being cranked all over the field, we were ready to crank some St. Regis punks into the field. Their bench-players and fielders roared toward us and we tackled them with double-leg takedowns. I was a fire burning through any log of flesh in a different colored uniform, my face and eyes demon red, but a mass of human debris piled up between me and Bassoli and I couldn't reach him. Coaches, umpires and parents yelled at us to stop but we couldn't. We kept hissing and yanking at limbs until, at last, giant Jonathan Van Runig rumbled over from first base.

We insects scurried because we didn't want to get stomped. Jonathan was six-foot-nine and three hundred and seventy pounds. Too slow to play basketball, or even to anchor the offensive line for the football team, he could hit a baseball so far it'd get arrested if it weren't carrying a passport. We all knew the Yankees had invited him to numerous try-outs and rumor had it his father Big Dutch was negotiating a contract. Nobody was about to shoot a double-leg takedown on Jonathan. It'd be like trying to tackle a tree. If he fell forward and landed on you, you'd die.

He was carrying a bat too, my bat, which I'd dropped when I'd fallen to the ground due to the baseball fired at my skull. I loved that bat. It was the lucky bat I'd won in a raffle at the previous season's team banquet, the night my teammates voted me captain, and it had been good for a lot of line-drives into the gap. Now Van Runig was wielding it like a policeman's riot baton and our second baseman Rupert Delfino panicked and took off running. Unfortunately for Rupert, his act of fleeing caught Van Runig's attention and caused the mutant to chase after him, still waving my lucky bat. There was no way Rupert would ever get caught – he was quick and scared to death and Van Runig sprinted with the blinding speed of an iceberg – still the sight of that huge kid chasing anyone with a bat was so horrifying, so pregnant with the potential of battered bones and Rupert dead two weeks before prom that the rest of us stopped fighting.

For long moments Rupert scampered in manic figure-eights deep into rightfield and Van Runig lurched after him impossibly slowly, like one of those claymation monsters from the *Sinbad* movies. We couldn't help but cheer – all of us, from both teams, except maybe for Bassoli – for tiny Rupert to escape. Three police cars zoomed off the street, sirens huge and round and echoing off the bleachers, and they flashed right past us, all of them speared toward right-center. They skidded and stopped in a circle surrounding Rupert and Van Runig, enclosing them like two coliseum combatants except Van Runig was the lion and Rupert wasn't even a Christian, more like some Christian's terrified pet rodent. The sirens switched off and we could hear one of the cops bellow through a bullhorn: "Put the bat on the ground, son. Put the bat down now."

The big kid halted his chase, breathing hard like he was about to pass out, and laid my lucky bat tenderly in the grass. Rupert kept running. Slipped past the police cars and bee-lined across centerfield, hopping the fence and disappearing into the dark woods beyond. Big Dutch ambled out to rightfield to negotiate with the police – to tell them to go easy, his son had a shot with the Yankees – and one of the cops confiscated my bat. I never saw it, or three hits in one game, ever again.

Maybe it's because I never had the chance to tackle Bassoli that he doesn't recognize me now, and why I still have the urge to drive a fist into his doughy chin. I restrain myself and rise from my desk as he offers one of his pudgy pancake hands. "Excuse my wheezing," he says. "I got a chronic chest injury."

"Sorry to hear that. Have a seat."

"Yeah, freak thing. Took my kid fishing in Florida two summers ago and we were cruising upriver, going maybe twenty knots, and a sturgeon jumped out of the water and smacked into my chest. I almost died."

A chronic chest injury from a *sturgeon?*

What kind of bullshit is this?

This, Mr. Bassoli, is *my* classroom, *my* homefield. My desks that I polish each afternoon with Windex. My laminated posters of parts of speech, of what kinds of infractions constitute plagiarism, of Malcolm X. I called you in, sir, to talk about your son's inappropriate behavior, not to hear some fish story.

"Nah, for real," he says, gesturing with his blubbery fingers.

"Thing was a monster, like two hundred pounds. Knocked me unconscious. I was lucky as hell I didn't die. Fell backward into the boat instead of the river. Ronnie had to get us to shore and find the harbormaster to call an ambulance. Damn fish broke three ribs and bruised both lungs. I can hardly walk now. Got, like, a dent in my chest. I got a tattoo though to cover it, of a big leaping sturgeon. Want to see?"

I do. Yeah, very much.

Want to see the dude's brilliant fish tattoo on his fat hairy chest. I mean, how often do you get to see something like that?

Guy stands up from the desk where he's been sitting, a tricky maneuver since he's so bulky, and unzips his jacket. He's wearing a turtleneck and it takes him a minute to struggle out of it, like he's trying to pop the meat of an avocado out of its skin using only his thumbs. With the shirt at last over his head, he stands before me with a chest creamy and off-white and dented, a barrel of stomach-flesh jiggling over his belt. The tattoo is phenomenal. An eighteen-inch masterpiece of luminous blue and green and silver, its tail an arrow of muscle, its mouth open and fierce with sharp teeth. It is leaping in the way only animals in the wild can leap, free and glorious, celebrating the miracle of its own sleekness.

Anthony Bassoli stands in my classroom, wheezing, proud and shirtless, for at least a minute. He stretches his arms over his head and the fish appears to leap higher, to lunge for the sky through the watery flesh of his chest.

"That's amazing," I say. "That's the greatest tattoo I've ever seen."

He doesn't smirk. Not once. Just pulls his turtleneck on and sits back down.

"I can't hardly walk no more," he says. "My breathing hurts like somebody rapped me with a two-by-four. Damn right I better get something out of that fish."

I almost feel sorry for him, think about shaving the left half of my head and getting my own tattoo on my scalp. A dark black baseball with red stripes and orange flames around it, maybe swords or daggers spinning out of its hide, a storm of blood and broken bones dripping from the laces. His son Ronald smirks. Often. In ugly sneering fashion. He's the worst kid in all my classes. None of the other students like him.

When he strutted into my classroom day one, I knew he'd be trouble. He was his dad's height and exactly what people mean when they use the word wiry. His hands were big and thick like his father's, but the rest of him was one straight line of frenetic energy. He couldn't stay seated. Got up every five minutes to throw a crumpled piece of paper in the trash can, or to make a hocking noise in his throat and spit out the window. Sometimes to sharpen a pencil he never seemed to actually use. I looked up his profile on the computer, found lousy grades throughout his freshman and sophomore years. A bunch of art classes that hinted at an offbeat interest or a different learning style, but D's and F's in them too. Attendance issues. Anthony Bassoli listed as his father. No contact information for any other parent.

"Forgive my asking," I say to Anthony, "but Ronald's mom?"

He waves his hand in dismissive fashion, like an umpire who's signaling an obvious ball four. "Nah, not around."

"Does he have problems outside of school? Does he ever talk to you about what's on his mind?"

"He talks all the time. He's a good talker. Works for me at the garage. Cleans the vehicles. The taxis, I mean. I got a fleet. Crusader Cabs. You seen 'em?"

"Of course." Everybody knows about Crusader Cabs. An armada of maroon Cadillacs with ornate white crucifixes on the doors. Popular on Sundays. Shuttle people to and from church. Slightly higher rates but never late when bringing you to the airport.

I'm a Jew. I call them all the time. "I didn't know that was your company."

"Seven years now. Ronnie's a good worker. Never gives me any trouble. Saved my life, that kid."

"Ever see him do his homework?"

"He does his homework."

Not for my class, he doesn't. Doesn't do a damn thing. Just smirks and plays with his long fingers when I give the students an in-class writing assignment. I stare at him to let him know I'm noticing his lack of effort — my best I-see-you-and-you're-not-cutting-it-young-man glare — but he just smirks more, then crumples the blank piece of paper on his desk and gets up and throws it in the garbage. In the midst of one trip back to his seat during a quiz about images of decay in *All Quiet on the Western Front,* he clamped one of his hands on Deanna Torrence's shoulder, close to her neck, and whispered into her hair. She smiled uncomfortably and tried to move his hand, and he said something that made her suck her teeth and shake her head like a wet dog. Then he slapped her pen to the floor.

"Ronald," I said. "Outside, right now."

The most tangible thing I learned in teacher preparation school was never to give a disruptive kid an audience. That's what the disruptive kid wants, the chance to show his classmates how much of a badass he is by challenging his teacher. He'll never back down in front of his peers, so the thing to do is to isolate him, remove him from any situation where he's on stage, and then disarm him by trying to have a civil conversation. First, you talk about something else to diffuse the tension. Then, after you've established the dynamic of a human-to-human discussion, essentially of two people having coffee, that's when you work your way back to the issue and let the kid know what you want him to do.

This second half of the equation, the disarming part, is nearly as important as the isolating part, and I'm generally pretty good at diffusing tension. I try to pay to attention to what extracurricular activities a kid's involved in so when I get him out in the hallway, instead of scolding him right away, I can surprise him with *how's the hockey season going* or *I hear your band's got a gig at the teen center, is that this weekend,* but with Ronald, who'd been pulling his garbage for weeks, I did the one thing a teacher's never supposed to do. I launched right into him and escalated the conflict.

"You are flat disrespecting me in my classroom," I shouted, my face six inches from his, my spit misting the air between us. "Your behavior's immature and unacceptable. You need to shape the hell up right now, or you need to not be in this class. What's your choice?"

He was taller than I was, with those long rangy arms and big hands, but I'd kept wrestling all through college, and in amateur tournaments for years after that. My forearms are hammers. "Well," I continued, "what's it gonna be? Got anything to say?"

He didn't. Or probably he did, but he was afraid to say it. He curled his lips into a snarl and his whole face began to twitch, the electricity of his live-wire body heating his mouth and below his eyes so the bottom part of his face looked like the narrow snout of a rat. He clenched and unclenched his right fist and his eyes fluttered and watered and I knew he wanted to hit me. He wanted to take a swing and I hungered for him to try it. I didn't care about my teaching career. I didn't care about Sandra at home relying on my income so she could keep studying for her masters. All I cared about was that smirking, snarling teenager and how if he swung, I would elbow him dead in his jaw, leg-whip him to the ground and pound the back of his head until he bled.

Then Ronnie backed down, shook his twitching face, turned and ran off down the hallway. "I'm calling your father tonight," I yelled after him. "You will not re-enter this classroom until you decide you know how to behave with respect."

"So, what's the problem with my kid?" Bassoli says.

The problem's that he sports the same smirk you did on the pitcher's mound. The problem's that on hot afternoons when

I'm walking across baseball fields, the left side of my head still throbs. The problem is I lost my lucky bat, turned to wrestling, and years later wanted your son to try and punch me so I could kill him. "The problem," I say, "is that he's disruptive in class and unfocused. Is there anything wrong at home? Something bothering him?'

"Not that I know about."

We're quiet. Behind Anthony Bassoli, the poster of Malcolm X stares at me. Those sharp square glasses and that enormous long finger pointed like a sword.

"Whatever happened to Jonathan Van Runig?" I say. "I know he never made it with the Yankees."

Bassoli's puzzled. Pats a hand against his chest as if he's having a heart attack, then makes another dismissive fanning motion in the air. "You knew Johnny Giant?"

"I grew up around here. Everybody knew who he was."

Bassoli stares at me and I think something might be clicking. There's a spark of anger in his eyes, a twitch of facial fat around his mouth. "He's upstate now," he says, his voice thin. "Corrections officer. Busts heads with a nightstick."

"Ronald scares people," I say, leaning in so my face is closer to Bassoli's. "He intimidates other students and he behaves disrespectfully toward me."

"Ronnie's a good kid."

"I'm not saying he isn't. Just that he needs to control himself in class. Needs to respect the learning environment. Can you talk to him about it?"

"I came here to talk to you."

His finger jabs at me like Malcolm X's and he angles forward. Our faces, separated by two desks, do all they can to push to about a foot apart. It's one thing to think about beating on his son, but this man is a whale. A whale with a fish tattooed on his dented chest. "I took off work," he says. "Had to pay overtime to my assistant dispatcher."

"You want to hit me?" I say.

"I hit you already," he says, tapping a fat thumb against his left temple. "Right here."

I remember this about the pitch. Even though it flew at me too fast to avoid, everything still slowed. There was the smirk, the giggle, the wind-up and then the release. I was focused on his hand, my eyes like zoom lenses on the ball as it left his fingertips. I could feel my weight shifting, first slightly back, then the gathering and push forward, the whole force of my body mustered to strike.

The standard way people teach hitting is to coach the batter to watch the bat hit the ball, to keep your eyes locked on the pitch until the moment of impact. But it doesn't really happen like that. The bat and ball intersect too quickly for the human eye to follow. What happens is the ball starts off small when it's released some fifty-five feet away. It appears to grow bigger until it reaches the point along its arc where it's most visible to the batter. At that moment, the hitter estimates what trajectory the rest of the ball's flight will travel and tries to time his swing to intersect with that trajectory, while the ball simultaneously passes that maximum field of vision and appears to diminish in size. Hence, when balls dip or curve with late breaks, they're extremely difficult to hit.

A batter knows the ball is headed to his face when it never shrinks, when it appears to keep growing until a massive blur slams his skull. That's what I remember most, the spherical avalanche overwhelming my entire sense of sight just before the smack.

Anthony Bassoli, on the other hand, has been crippled by a fish he never saw coming. "This is stupid," I say. "All that was twenty years ago."

"So why are you still taking it out on my son?"

Unlike his pitches, particularly the one aimed at my head, this assessment is not accurate. Ronald Bassoli is a behavior problem. Not just in my classroom either. Other teachers have told me about his drawing pictures of rifles on desks, about his throwing books at the whiteboard and cursing at authority figures that confront him. "I lost my lucky bat that day," I say. "I never hit consistently after that."

"Not my kid's fault."

"No, it's not."

We're stuck in mud. Two tough dump-trucks with rusted under-carriages and noxious diesel fuel and our front bumpers too close to each other to maneuver, our wheels useless. I watch him and wonder if he'll admit his kid's a screw-up. I could end this right now, tell him all right, it's just a misunderstanding, tomorrow's a new day. As long as Ronnie comes to class smiling and prepared, and I'll give him another chance. But I don't tell Bassoli anything, I just sit there, behind my bulky teacher's desk with the box of tissues on it, and the stapler and the gradebook, and I watch him. I just sit there and wait.

"You had too much mouth," he says. "That's why we hated you. All your yapping from the outfield."

I don't respond. In teacher school, the technique is called wait time. Give the student enough room to figure out what he wants to say. Don't interrupt and try to guide the conversation.

"It was respect, you know. We hit you because you were the only guy on your team who could threaten us."

I hold back and wait some more. It's difficult. I think of Rupert, how he disappeared into the woods. How two weeks later, at prom, we teased him without rest and he got drunk and we kicked him out of the limo and left him passed out on his front lawn. When his brother tried to drag him into the shower, Rupert punched him and broke his glasses. Kid showed up to his ninth grade English class the next day with a gauze bandage roofing one eye like a pirate.

"Everything I've done bad in my life I've paid for," Bassoli says. "My wife left me. A sturgeon beat my lungs to shit. I'm not apologizing for anything."

Is that what I'm after? An apology? I doubt it. I spent too many years shoving noses into the mat to care whether people are sorry for what they do. "Show me your tattoo," I say. "I want to see your tattoo again."

He's not nearly as proud this time. Pushes up from his desk as if I'd just asked him to read a passage of Shakespeare aloud, as if he'd like to run me over with one of his cabs. His undress is quicker, less dramatic. Some facial fat twitches. When his chest is bare though, this time he can't help but smirk. He knows what he's got.

The fish is a luminous spire in full breach. A dazzling aquatic angel ascending, propelling itself skyward by the torque of its own magnificent thrust. I try to imagine what it saw as it leapt, how big Bassoli's chest grew in its eyes. I try to imagine the incalculable timing that led to the collision of sturgeon and father, the collision that left a dent.

"Lift your arms," I say.

"Make it jump," I say.

He does.

ON THE CASE

You tell Daniel you think somebody stole a box of Pop Tarts from your backseat because, well, who else are you gonna tell?

Not your wife. You don't want her to know you bought Pop Tarts from the Safeway, or that you ever buy them, not with your stomach starting to push like a soccer ball against the skin of your shirt. You can't tell your kids either because you don't want them thinking buying Pop Tarts is a legitimate way to spend money after you refused them the Pokemon treasure chest and the GameCube. So who else can you tell? The cops? You're gonna report a Grand Theft Pop Tart?

You tell Daniel at work because you know he'll think it's funny, he'll laugh with you, but he'll take it seriously too.

"Are you telling me someone jacked Pop Tarts from your car?" he says.

"Yeah, man a double-box. Sixteen pastries."

"What flavor?"

"Strawberry."

"Frosted?"

"Dude, of course."

"That's messed up, man," Daniel says. "People are messed up. What are you gonna do?"

"I'm not gonna do anything. It's Pop Tarts. Should I, like, red alert the FBI?"

"You could call Safeway and complain. Say they need more security in the parking lot. Demand they replace the box for you."

This is what you love about Daniel. He always finds a weasel third way to deal with problems. That's why the two of you are the best sales team at the network, why you've won a free cruise every year for hitting your quotas. You were about to close a huge deal last week with Cypress Mineral Water when some stuck-up budget skank in their conference room started tapping her pen on the leather-bound proposal and whining about how it's not enough primetime spots, and the Q-factor of the Thursday night sitcom is too low to generate the viewership of twenty-something females they want buying their bullshit over-priced fake water, and you were ready to reach over and smack her designer granny glasses straight through her eyeballs when Daniel said, Hold on, what if we talk to the writers? What if we have them write in a new love interest for our tragi-comic hero and she's this totally buffed rock climber with arms like lithe muscular snakes and we'll do some product placement and every time he talks to her, she'll zing hip witty comments and show off her guns and her beautiful flowing hair and she'll be holding a cold dewy bottle of Cypress? How's that sound?

And now you're making reservations for expensive berths on the boat going from San Juan to Porlamar, and it'll be just like it's been for the past three years. The kids will eat their heads off and attend day-camps starring Midwestern undergrads as warm and welcoming counselors, and Emily will play suntan and volleyball, and you and Daniel will do what you always do – beer, beer, and additional beer except there will be more of it, and better potato skins with grease that's creamier and more luxurious and then the best part, the chugging forward through ocean as if you're riding a grand carving knife splitting the watery seam of the world, and even though the waves will re-fold and heal themselves you will have made a cut in something so much bigger than you, something that could swallow you and not even taste you in its spit.

"Listen," you say to Daniel, "I think I know who did it."

You tell him how when you parked, there was a woman pulling garbage bags filled with cans and bottles out of what looked like a thirty-year-old Lincoln. It was rusted around the tire-wells and inside her trunk a large spool of yellow nylon rope lay on its side, surrounded by a half-dozen bruised and misshapen bleach-jugs that looked like they'd been used to pummel someone's skull. She was maybe five-foot-four with brittle grey hair, blue jeans with oil stains and a lumpy lime-green sweatshirt with an ironed-on portrait of Dora the Explorer. Her face looked red and pissed-off as if she'd just lost a fight.

Shit, you thought, maybe I should lock the car, but you didn't because you hate locking your car and it was your second trip to Safeway that morning. You bought the Pop Tarts on the first trip and you forgot to pick up the toothpaste and tofu you were supposed to get, so now you had to stop back there, and you were irritated because who wants to go to the supermarket twice in one day, and why does your wife apparently believe tofu is the answer to every damn thing wrong with the world, and so, screw it, you didn't lock the car.

But you did open the rear passenger door and reach in to shoulder your computer bag, and the woman saw you, and she knew damn well you only grabbed your laptop because you thought she might steal it and she looked at you like she would like to batter you with one of those bleach bottles, so when you returned to your car and the Pop Tarts had vanished from the back seat, you figured she just took them out of spite.

"Dude," Daniel says, "I think we can catch her."

What would you do if you caught her? Beat her ass? Demand restitution? But you let Daniel spill his idea because he seems excited about it, rotating back and forth on his spinning desk-chair as if he's a kid at an ice cream parlor, and when he's finished he flips you his smirk which says damn right I closed the deal, and you realize his plan actually makes sense.

Later, after the staff meeting and a bout of unsuccessful cold-calling, and lunch with the people from the discount furniture chain which looks like it might lead to something promising even though you hate their revolting cheerleader jingle – *couches, coffee-tables, touch-lamps more/ let us decorate your living-room floor* –

you give Daniel the thumbs-up and you can see him giggling as he jots down notes from the city's web site that will tell you which neighborhoods will be flaunting their recyclable materials curbside tonight.

The two of you lean over your desk like a couple of hardcore analysts from the slaughter-all-the-terrorists weekly drama that's the network's highest rated Sunday night hour, and you glance to the corner of your office and try to channel the steely gaze of the life-sized plastic model of John Benson, the show's twice-divorced, sometimes coke-addicted hero. The thing is essentially a six-foot-tall doll, and he stands before you, arms crossed beneath his train-car pectorals, with a silver pistol poking from his waistband like a gleaming erection. You stare down Benson's empty eyes and his hyper-masculine carriage reenergizes something vital in your chin-cleft and you and Daniel huddle over the map he downloaded. You participate in several minutes of squinting and nodding, plot makeshift parabolas and hypotenuses, then decide, yes, it's got to be the area known as Lower Edgar Park. That's the closest neighborhood to the Safeway, the neighborhood with the most houses with the most children who drink the most soda and the most bottled water – and the most dads, like you, with beer-fridges in their garages – and that's where she'll be tonight.

"I'll come by your place at midnight," Daniel says. "She won't be out before that. Recycling pirates wait until everybody's asleep, then they creep out and lurk. Then they skulk around and plunder the bins."

You like that Daniel called them pirates. Skulkers instead of scavengers. As if they're committing a despicable unlawful act, not just trying to survive by sifting through other people's garbage. The pirate label makes you feel better about trying to apprehend one of them, as if, well, if you don't draw the line here, what will she do next? Cans and bottles to Pop Tarts. Pop Tarts to wallets and jewelry and firearms. This is a nation of laws and nobody's above them. Daniel's getting way too excited though, speaking in a near-whisper about how he's going to ride up on his bike and how you should have your bike ready too, how the night will be a slow cruise, kind of a mobile stake-out from block to block, and how it would never work with a car because you'd make too much noise and spook her.

"Dude, hold on," you say, thinking how Daniel's got no wife or children so he shouldn't just make assumptions about your availability for this kind of adventure, even though Emily and the kids will already be asleep so it won't be a problem for you to sneak out. "Listen," you tell him, "I'm up for this, but if you show up in a black turtleneck and a watch-cap, I'm gonna beat you with a bucket."

He doesn't. Just a navy windbreaker and a backward Dodgers hat, and some eye-black under his eyes as if the streetlights might blind him, but you don't say anything because you're excited too. You even spent twenty minutes in the garage spraying WD-40 on your gears and chain to minimize squeaking, and you set your phone to vibrate on the off-chance your father with the emphysemic wheeze will die and somebody will call to tell you at two in the morning. When you swing your legs over your bike like the Caped Crusader hopping into the Batmobile, Daniel has to reach out and grab your arm. "It's a slow cruise, remember?" he says. "We need to sneak up on her while she's in the midst of her thievery. We need to swoop like silent owls. She looks up and, wow, where'd those guys come from? Got it?"

You're not much of a swooper. You are line-backer beefy, a bulldozer. Yet you nod at Daniel in a manner that's serious because, yes, tonight, you will lance the night with silent grace.

For the first hour, you see nothing. Not the lady. Not any other recycling pirates. Just two teenagers having the kind of forty-five-minute break-up fight that should take thirty seconds, one inside the car brooding, the other outside on her driveway with numerous violent-looking gestures and a loud fuck you that resonates like a church bell off the high roofs of the surrounding cul-de-sac.

What you're doing feels spiritual. You're riding bikes like two tactical assassins, cruising slow and quiet through the dark, all senses on high alert. The night is warm and calm, there's the faint echo of hip hop beats from the basement of a house with a glowing silver ball like a miniature moon shining amidst a driveway's leafy hedge. Large screen TVs push purple and blue specters through picture windows and you glide right through them. You feel the air streaming around you as you pedal. You are swooping. You have been designed aerodynamically, not for sales, not for beer, not for husbandry or parenting, but for this slow cruise astride your bicycle. You bless that woman for stealing your Pop Tarts. She has given you this night, this liquid panther-stalk through your city. People are not messed up. People just need to get out more, need to lube their chains and glide.

Both you and Daniel are surprised when you see her. You have long trusted Daniel's genius, but this is something different. Predicting human behavior when you're sitting across the table from someone in a conference room is one thing. Knowing what a woman he's never seen will be doing past one in the morning, and where she'll be doing it, approaches the level of prophet. "Holy shit," Daniel says, as if he's scared too. "There she is."

She's half a block away, across the street, shuffling beneath a streetlight. You and Daniel stop pedaling and roll a little closer, angling behind a large SUV to stow your bikes. You crouch down near the front bumper so you can watch her, and as long as you're quiet, she won't spot you. Daniel moves into position behind you and you could be two dudes at a Bar Mitzvah in a conga line, except his hands aren't on your hips and you'd punch him in the eye if they were.

The woman has replaced her Dora sweatshirt with a maroon raincoat, but it looks like she's wearing the same grease-stained jeans. There's a rhythm to her pushing, a right-left shove forward, a pause, a hover of dead space, a right-left shove forward, a pause. She's got three shopping carts strung together with her nylon cord, and the bottles of bleach are knotted along the rope too, situated as buffers between the carts to muffle the jangle when she shoves forward and they smack against each other. The cart she's pushing is full and the one in front of it almost full, the lead cart empty. She's close to two-thirds of the way through her mission.

What do you want to call what she's pushing? A makeshift junk-jalopy vacuum? A recycling freight-train? Performance art? She's pilfering trash bins, but she's also a kind of social engineer. The cardiovascular architect of Lower Edgar Park. She's a sieve, thinning the neighborhood's refuse, siphoning glass, aluminum and plastic nickel-nuggets, and re-injecting the discarded wealth into the blood of the city. She's guiding a mobile laboratory, a shopping cart IV drip, and she halts it expertly with the mostly filled middle cart parallel to the next bin she investigates. Most bottles and cans she shuttles quickly from bin to cart, but when she encounters a product she's unfamiliar with, she raises it to the streetlight and examines it like a jeweler, searching for the hieroglyph that will reveal its value. It's when she lifts a bottle that you recognize as being from Cypress' newest line of fruit-flavored water — which tastes mostly like sugared sewage — that something else nags at her attention. She gazes back at the house she just passed, where she didn't stop her junk-lab because whoever ferries the trash out — probably an overworked new father who'll wake up at four to schlep it to the curb — hasn't done the job yet.

For a moment she rolls the revolting Cypress bottle in her hands as if she's considering something novel that just occurred to her, then she dumps it into her cart and finishes sifting through the rest of the bin. Before she shuffles on, she leaves her plunder-bus at the curb and creeps across the front lawn toward the porch of the house she studied moments earlier.

Daniel grabs your sleeve. "Dude," he whispers, "we gotta stop her. She's trespassing."

"So?'

"She's crossed the threshold from curb to yard. Anything

can happen now. What if she breaks into the house and stabs someone?"

You consider this, but don't move. The woman steps quietly onto the porch.

"Stop her," Daniel hisses, but he doesn't yell, and neither do you. She appears to move a few things around the porch, then grabs the handle of a jogging stroller, wheels it around, and pushes it down the stairs.

"Yo, she's stealing that," Daniel says.

"You don't know that," you say.

"She just crept up to that porch and snatched it. Are you blind? That's her, right there, pushing it down the walkway."

"Maybe she has a kid at home and she's thinking of buying a new stroller, did you ever think of that? Maybe she just wants to test this one on the street, see if she likes the feel of it. A woman like her who pushes stuff around all the time, she's probably a discerning consumer."

"A discerning consumer? Are you fucking kidding me? She stole your Pop Tarts. Now she's stealing the stroller. She's a thief."

Daniel's right. There's no third way here. The woman's affixing the stroller to the front cart, weaving the yellow twine around the handle to secure it. It's an expensive model, a status-stroller, sleek and triangular with a lightweight aluminum frame that's collapsible for easy stowage when traveling. No way you could have afforded it when your kids were of stroller age. The family with the front porch will wake tomorrow and want to take their kid to the park, probably a wailing infant who needs to get outside, needs some time away from the house, and from Mommy who's been nursing him for seven hours straight, and Daddy will volunteer for the job in order to keep his marriage afloat and he'll pack the diaper bag, fill the sippy cup, get ready to earn some serious sensitive-male points with his wife and when he goes to garner the vanished stroller – whoops, oh boy – the recriminations will be loud and enduring because Mommy has told Daddy repeatedly not to leave the stroller on the porch, to store it in the garage because hasn't he noticed stuff disappearing from their yard every once in a while? Little stuff like the snow shovel that one time in the winter, and whatever happened to the Frisbee?

Yeah, he'll say, but who's cruel enough to steal a stroller? And who's bold enough to venture all the way onto their porch?

Once again, you minimized my concerns, she'll say, you never take me seriously, and he'll shout, Don't make this a bigger deal than it is, you always blow everything out of proportion, and the baby will be wailing and the whole weekend will be ruined, and maybe their marriage too.

"Do something," Daniel says, because even though he's the genius, you're the muscle. That's what makes your team work. He does his let-me-appeal-to-your-inner-weasel thing, and then you step forward with the papers, holding them with your meat-hook hand, your lead-pipe arm and GQ smile, and the subtle undertone of *we just spent our whole afternoon talking to you and if you end up wasting our time maybe you shouldn't be too confident about your legs or your jawbone or your windshield*, and the deal closes and it's time to start making reservations for the cruise.

Daniel's right. You should stop her because even though you don't give a shit about that couple's marriage – they'll be fine with their too big house with the fake Victorian eaves and the satellite dish, and they'll have a new stroller, a more chic model with an even lighter alloy by this afternoon – still, there's the broken window theory to consider. If you don't stop the woman from jacking the stroller, what will she steal next? Maybe, you'll wake one morning and there will be empty space on the street where your car slept happily the night before.

"Do something," Daniel says again, almost whimpering now. At heart Daniel's a wuss and if you don't do something, there's no way he will, but you don't do anything, because the woman's moving again with her rhythmic right-left shuffle push and the night is warm and calm, and the stroller affixed to the front cart looks like the sharp prow of a ship, and you're thinking of the boat you'll be on in two weeks, of the beer, of so much beer, and of the ocean unfolding, and there she goes, there she goes, cutting her way through the dark.

SCRAMBLE

The summer Gordon and Lennie christened me Eugene was the summer Gordon was beautiful. His muscles were fresh and newly defined, miracles in the way muscles can only be the first time, when they surprise.

He was slim and strong, his hair thick and dark. He carried thirty-pound golf bags casually, a bit disdainfully, as if they were schoolbooks. The skin on his face, and from his elbows through his hands, was the brown of wet beach-sand. Girls from our class pedaled their bicycles to his front porch in the early evenings and told him how many stuffed animals they still slept with, and how they liked to be held when they kissed.

On a Monday night in August, he showed me an unrolled condom on the bookshelf in his bedroom. Used, he said.

I wouldn't see another used condom for seven years.

That summer, I was as ugly as a fourteen-year-old can be, a sickening combination of short and pudgy, with limbs that were long and gangly. I looked like a potato an angry infant had jabbed toothpicks into for arms and legs. My head was oblong, my hair angled wrong and brittle, still cut by the half-drunk barber who'd once dated my mother. My teeth stuck out like thumbs, held in check by painful railroad tracks that cut my gums and glommed onto food-crumbs as if they had tentacles, infusing my breath with the stench of rotting vegetables. Horrible qualities for anybody, but excruciating for a kid so consistently horny, he walked around with a boner three or four times each hour.

I had nowhere to put that boner, no idea at all what to do with it, and its nagging presence distracted and embarrassed me. I tried to hide it with long t-shirts or by offering three-quarters of my back during conversations. People thought I was rude, but I was just trying to be considerate, attempting to shield friends and strangers both from my rancid breath and the inappropriate bump in my boxers.

Gordon and Lennie and I, and another dude named Horace, played a lot of cards that summer. Horace wasn't Jewish and didn't caddy because he had a job washing dishes in a deli that made dry-tasting sandwiches with too much meat. We gathered on the screened-in back-porch at Lennie's house and his mother fed us Hostess cupcakes and off-brand potato chips and pitchers of fruit punch mixed from foil packets. She'd say, "How about some brownies? Or should I cook that homemade pizza you like, Len?" and he'd shout at her, "We're good, Ma, for real. Just leave us alone."

We laughed at Lennie and told his mom to keep the food coming, which she did, so we ate a lot, if not well, and we grew even though we were burning roughly four million calories a day carrying golf bags. Because we worked at a country club with a lot of douchebag members – including Lennie's parents who were members but not douchebags – we were obsessed with Matt Dillon's cabana-boy role in *The Flamingo Kid*. We wanted to be self-assured and knowing like he was so girls and older married women would want to do us, even if Gordon was the only one who knew what doing anyone meant. Like Dillon, we wanted to be familiar with the slick universe of playing cards, wanted to be able to recognize when people who tried to scam us were cheating or bluffing, wanted to be able to shuffle decks with quick and practiced confidence. We played poker sometimes, but the money we made caddying felt too precious to risk losing – especially to each other – so mostly our game was spades. Gordon, the best player, was handicapped with me because I was the worst, and that made it fair against Lennie and Horace.

If you could only bet one book, you had to proclaim you were betting the donger. It was silly and demeaning, but even though we didn't actually wager money, or maybe because of that, the biggest sin anyone could make was to under-bet. That wasn't playing by the rules of the cool, confident personas we were crafting for ourselves — being feckless and conservative was for the half-dead geezer-schmucks whose bags we carried — so if you absolutely had to bet only one book, you had to claim the donger, and then you had to unzip your pants and play the whole hand with your package hanging out beneath the table. This prospect caused obvious problems for me because every time Mrs. Ross asked if we wanted more food, which was every fifteen minutes, the sound of her voice caused me to pop a rod.

I spent a lot of time in that house with my back turned to Lennie's mother, who wore tight capris and bright flowered blouses over her water-balloon breasts and, fortunately, never seemed to notice my rudeness because she was enthralled by Gordon and the ripples in his shoulders. Still, because my strategy was to avoid at all costs the potential problems that could ensue from betting the donger, I never under-bet, I *over-bet*. I'd have a hand with worse than nothing and I'd wager three books and we'd get crushed and Gordon would glare at me and mutter, "Jesus, Eugene, what are you, retarded?"

Now, two decades later, Gordon's face is repulsive. He addresses the ball on the first tee and grimaces, looking pissed and vicious during his takeaway as he twists the over-engorged muscles in his back. I don't understand how he retains any flexibility at all with his massive weightlifter's build. He looks like a cartoon bad guy. His jaw's still square, but his neck and shoulders are so thick his head is tiny in comparison, like a grapefruit on a gorilla. A hairless gorilla. With his bald dome and small, angry eyes, he could be a Neo-Nazi setting out with a lead-pipe to stalk the streets, but he's only trying to hit a golf ball. He crushes it two-hundred-and-eighty yards down the middle of the fairway, which is roughly sixty yards farther than I've ever hit anything in my life. Lisa and

Natalie, the two attractive women on the tee with us, applaud and nod as if they understand something significant, and Gordon claps me on the shoulder and says, "All right, partner, I played it safe. Go ahead and rip it."

Gordon's clap on the shoulder is, in fact, a slap in the face. He knows I've never ripped anything. The asshole's messing with me before I even start my round. He's well aware that playing it safe is as much a part of my daily survival strategy as the trio of breath mints I still pop every half-hour, that the only bravado I've ever displayed was when we played spades and even that was counterfeit, the desperate pose of a faux maverick attempting to avoid an erection-related catastrophe. Yet here he is, taunting me when the two most beautiful women who've ever paid attention to me in the bleak history of me are actually watching me, focusing on me, actually caring about what my physical body is capable of doing.

I muster the dignity necessary to attempt only a single practice swing, flex my back muscles as if I have some, and then drub the ball forty feet, a weak grounder to the right side, barely nudging past the ladies' tee. Technically, it doesn't matter how lousy my shot is because it's a scramble tournament and we'll only play the best of our four drives – I'll just have to pick mine up – but I'm terrified Gordon will make a comment about how I just missed having to play a "dick-out" hole. A dick-out hole is an adult variant of our teenage card games. If you fail to get your drive past the ladies' tee, you have to unzip and play the rest of the hole with your package jauntily swinging, but Gordon doesn't say anything about that, just looks back with his shrunken monkey head and winks, and though I know his silence has less do with his growing up than with his not wanting to appear a total juvenile in front of two intelligent blond women in tight skirts with legs like race-horses, I think maybe I made the right decision in recruiting him for our team. This is the annual charity golf outing at my highly successful and hugely corporate law firm, and no squad I've ever previously been on has ever won so much as a raffle. Instead, my name has been associated with a slew of last-place finishes and once, a second-to-last, which actually felt worse because of how people congratulated me for it.

Mostly my teams have sucked because I suck. I'm heavier than dead weight, a fossilized rock that drags anyone I play with deep into a pit of soul-sucking tar. Worse, with the random way the firm hooks up the foursomes, I've actually never been lucky enough to be slotted with anybody good. Except this year, I have no idea why, but somehow I got thrown in with Lisa, who played varsity at Northwestern, and Natalie whose father is a scratch handicap and senior partner and who wanted his daughter to be the next Nancy Lopez. That didn't work out, but trust me, she still drums the Jesus out of the ball. Better luck, the other nebbish we were supposed to play with, Bob Horowitz – who's only a slightly worse golfer than I am – apparently experienced an intimate moment with a deer tick on Martha's Vineyard a couple weekends ago. We just found out yesterday he's feverish and debilitated with early symptoms of Lyme's Disease, so I called up Gordon who said he was busy, had "a lot of important shit to do, you know, but all right, Eugene, what the hell, I guess I owe you."

That long ago summer when my teeth were encased in metal, we were a year removed from our parents allowing our Bar Mitzvah money to kick-start personal savings accounts, ostensibly to teach us the value of money. We already valued money, however – we'd been born valuing it – and though we had no real place to spend what we had, we carried golf bags to augment our accounts. With the exception of Gordon, we had no girlfriends, and he never seemed to take his anywhere, just received them at his house like mail. Despite our Flamingo Kid aspirations, we had no need to buy anything, and no vision of wanting to purchase cars, college, or any other part of growing old we cared nothing about. Still, we loved the thrill of weekly sojourns to the bank to deposit

don't log enough billable hours because meetings with me, phone conversations with me, are quick and to the point.

I try to be socially adept. I try to spend time during each interaction being "the grease that keeps the ball-bearings bouncing" as my supervisor advises me to be, though I'm not even sure what ball-bearings are, let alone whether they bounce.

My standard interaction with a client starts with my offering some engaging witticism such as, "Hey, how's it going?" and then I'm pretty much tapped out. Because I specialize in divorces, I can't move on to "How're the wife and kids?" so what typically follows is a fetid, polluted-swamp silence that makes me doubt I actually began my morning by coating my tongue with several mint-flavored cleansing products designed to inoculate against bacteria. I've yet to master the kind of warm laughter that can fill up that silence, that can paint the room with cheery bonhomie and add an extra fifteen minutes of bullshit to the meeting. I don't know how to do joviality. Instead, for thirty seconds I fidget and make pathetic and futile faces begging the client to assume responsibility for greasing the ball-bearings. Inevitably, as the silence grows and threatens to suffocate the conference room, the building, the city, I panic. Too soon, I lick the insides of my teeth, and say, "Let's get down to business, shall we?"

My supervisor says I'm costing the firm a hundred grand a year. Minimum.

Women like Lisa and Natalie don't talk to me either, or they might initially out of politeness, but when the swamp silence hits, they pivot like ballerinas and make excuses about text messages, and Gordon knows all these shortcomings about me. He knows I often spend five out of seven nights a week wondering if I should shoot myself. That's why I'd like to brain him with a golf club right now, angle an eight-iron like a cleaver through his pea-sized skull, then leave him bleeding in the fairway.

I'm not surprised, after I demonstrate my proficiency to swing as hard as I can and nub golfballs roughly the length of my living room, that Lisa and Natalie have no use for me. They tolerate my slightly sweaty presence on the tee box, the uncomfortable mix of my perfumey cologne and over-medicated mouth, and my two-hundred dollar ill-fitting golf shirt and professionally pressed slacks while I address the ball, and they blandly expect horrible, uninspiring contact when I swing. After I fail to disappoint that expectation, they stoically move on. It makes sense for them to gallop like gazelles with those long tasty legs far ahead of me in the fairway while I hunt around in the high grass for my pathetic shots. But Gordon, he's supposed to be my friend. He's not supposed to be loping along with them, sandwiched between them as they laugh and joke as to whether the team should play Natalie's perfect shot, or Lisa's perfect shot, or Gordon's perfect shot. Maybe that's not even what they're talking about. Maybe the shot-choice is obvious and knowable to anyone not stuck excavating gnarly clumps of rough in hopes of not losing yet another six-dollar personally monogrammed golf ball. Maybe they're joking about something entirely different, something airy and hip and totally unrelated to the present moment. Either way, I have no access to their fun.

Gordon's supposed to stick with me in the muck and encourage me because it's still possible that at some crucial point in the round my skills will be vital to our team's success. He's supposed to buoy me with inanities like, "You just missed that one, buddy, but you'll come around, you always do," and he should be helping me find my ball. He's not supposed to be up ahead flirting, bopping along, admiring the curve of a laughing breast or the swish of a loping hip. That's not why I called him to play with us. I called Gordon instead of, say, Lennie, because Gordon's never betrayed me before. He's patient with me. He possesses reservoirs of patience. This is the same man who loved calling me retard, but who nonetheless never turned me down as his spades partner, never refused to play with me even though my breath reeked, even though I bet four books when I should have claimed the donger.

The caddyshack at Flintmoor was a tent. Inside it were benches and folding chairs but no tables, and never enough places for everybody to sit. If you didn't get there early enough, you had to stand. Sometimes for hours. The caddymaster, an obese man named Stan with a clean-shaven face who wore collared shirts and mud-hued slacks, sat nearby on a barstool in a small wooden booth like a toll collector. There he answered phones and charted tee-times and sold us Devil Dogs and Fanta Orange Sodas. When a coterie of members was ready to head to the tee, he'd squeeze out from his booth with a ballpoint pen behind his ear and a clipboard in his left hand. "Johnny Jones," he might say, pointing to one of the veterans who caddied as a career, moving south in the winter to work the clubs in Florida, "you got Stein and Bloom. Beal and Beal too. Two carts."

Johnny was Stan's favorite caddy, his drinking buddy who accompanied him to the chariot-racing track each night, and he always got the premium loops. Four bags on two carts was the best anyone could hope for – you just had to carry a quartet of putters and you made sixty bucks plus tips. Kids like me and Lennie never got loops like that, but we didn't begrudge the grizzled black men like Johnny and Sparks and Lester who did, with their broken knees and hand-me-down golf shoes. Johnny, who did way better than Stan at the track, had a car, an old Ford he kept polished and purring. The rest of the career guys bused it to the club, limping into the caddy tent with racing forms curled beneath one arm, clutching paper bags housing fried-egg-and-butter sandwiches on hard rolls. They talked to us about women, about the track, about how good they were as golfers in their own right. If you got paired up with any of them, they took care of you, telling you where to stand and what to look for on the course. Because they knew I was hapless, they'd even follow the ball into the woods if the person I was caddying for hit one there. They were being helpful and kind, sure, but they also knew if they covered for my fuck-ups, the round would go smoother, everyone would be happier, and they'd make more in tips.

I could have learned a lot from them if I'd been paying attention. I was the worst caddy in the tent. Poor Stan would look in my direction only when everyone else was already on the course. There'd be a reluctant hope in his eyes then, a kind of pleading that either I'd somehow do a better job, or I'd get so discouraged by my own incompetence that I'd stop showing up for work.

Gordon, on the other hand, was terrific. He was as good as the career caddies, better in some ways. He didn't know every nook of the course like they did, but he was a Jew and they weren't, so he knew the culture of the members more intimately. He knew how to make them comfortable with off-color jokes and he could talk politics with them. In his own way he was the Flamingo Kid, charming older men and women, making them want to adopt him as a son. They loved him because he personified no societal guilt. He was a bright young herald of the elders' own tribe and they could share wisdom in order to aid him along his journey – a marked contrast to the beaten-down, sometimes-smelling-like-liquor servants from another social class who wore golf shoes they'd discarded five years ago and literally bore the weight of their leisure on their backs.

Gordon was a fresh breath, standing unbuckled and handsome in the mist and dew of the fairways, and he could caddy for anybody, even Newfeld and Bloch.

We always knew when it was about to happen. Instead of squeezing from his booth and strutting to the front of the tent, belly puffed with his big boss status and the security of knowing he would never have to carry another bag except his own, Stan would shuffle out shamefacedly. He wouldn't gaze over the congregation searching out which of us to favor with the upcoming loop like a faith-healer choosing whom to grace with a miracle. Rather, he'd stretch his palms upward and say, "Okay who wants 'em? Newfeld and Bloch going out in fifteen minutes. Anybody?"

The older caddies would get real busy with their racing forms, or stare at the ground, or start rubbing their tired backs. Newfeld and Bloch were sons-of-bitches, the worst loop at the club. Legend had it they'd once caused Largeman George – a stellar caddy who'd reportedly carried for Tom Wieskopf at the U.S. Open – to lose his job when, overflowing with anger at the way they were treating him, he'd shrugged their bags off his shoulders in the middle of the eighteenth fairway, and then one at a time, hurled each magnificent over-stuffed trunk into the middle of the pond fronting the green. Then, without looking back, he'd walked off the course directly to the bus-stop.

The story is legendary because the launching of a member's bag into a pond constitutes a colossal and gorgeous gesture of defiance. It takes a powerful man to hurl a bag of clubs. There's the grip and heft, the momentum that must be generated to sail something that bulky through the air. The tricky timing of the toss. It's a feat worthy for competition in a World's Strongest Man contest, a feat that speaks of a surrounding clamor, a noisy chaos of country and culture that cannot be walled away by high fences and membership fees. Like sleeping with the prettiest girl in the senior class behind her boyfriend's back and giving her the best orgasm she's ever had, it's also the kind of triumph I will never accomplish in this lifetime. While I was getting yelled at during a loop, I liked to imagine what Largeman's launch might have looked like, the heavy bags soaring upward, individual clubs and balls tumbling into the water before the finality of the great massive splash.

Jonathan Newfeld and Ira Bloch both had high squeaky voices and had been either widowed or divorced. Regardless of the circumstances that ended their marriages, they seemed as socially inept as I was, except older and more venomous. They'd blame their caddies for every lousy shot they hit, which was every shot they hit. Heading out with them meant five hours of searching for balls in the woods and digging into clumps of poison ivy because the bitter bastards refused to ever give up on a ball. You'd troop back in after the loop with your feet blistered from your wet socks, and your legs and pants soaked because they'd made you wade into water hazards to retrieve the balls they'd dunked there, and you spent so much of the round raking sand traps that you felt like a landscaper. They'd yell at you constantly, screech that you were stupid and worthless if somehow your shadow had the temerity to intercept one of their shadows and then one of them shanked a ball into the trees. They were the undisputed kings of the miserable loop, walking cat-claws who never tipped a dime.

In fact, because they didn't want to feel guilty about never tipping, they successfully lobbied the club to adopt a no-tipping policy so no one else would tip either. Fortunately for us, the adoption of the policy actually increased how much money we made. First, to compensate for the absent tips, the club raised the rates from sixteen dollars a bag to eighteen, and second – except for when a caddy like me was the bungling boob holding the clubs – most of the members, who were generally douchebags of the paternalistic variety, kept tipping anyway. It seemed like they maybe even tipped more because the policy change made it a little illegal, a little naughty for them to dig into their pockets and fish out a billfold, to whisper, Hey, Caddy, here's for your troubles, and slide us a few bucks as if they were getting away with something.

This surreptitious tipping only further embittered Newfeld and Bloch and hardened their determination to be nasty and demeaning to whomever carried their bags. None of the veterans would do it. Gordon, who could wring a hefty tip out of anyone else, invariably stepped up. "I'll take 'em," he'd say, and the weathered veterans would shake their heads as if he were the stupidest moron on the planet.

But Gordon was playing a different angle. "If I take these clowns," he told me, "Stan will feel like he owes me. Watch what happens the rest of the week. I'll get out early and often. Two loops a day, sometimes three. I'll be getting loops with carts. Johnny Jones will always be number one, but check out who's gonna be number two. Just watch."

I did, and he was right. Gordon got loops before guys who'd been lugging bags for thirty years. Gordon got the big tipping couples like the Ginginfelds and the Sterns, who bought their caddies fat condiment-sloshed cheeseburgers at the snack-bar. Gordon got it all and his bank account doubled, then tripled, then quadrupled, all in one summer. He caddied for the biggest assholes at the club once a week, sucked up the miserable five hours without a tip, and the rest of the time he was golden. Stan loved him and the other caddies did too. He took the bullet for all of us.

It happens on the seventh hole. It's a par five and with Gordon's monster drive and Natalie's laser-stroked five-wood, we're on the fringe in two. Fifty feet from the cup. A birdie feels inevitable. I chip first so I can get my hack out of the way and let the others show off how close they can nestle the ball to the hole. That's my attitude when I line the shot up: just don't waste time, scurry through the motions and let one of your so-called teammates get the job done. Still, somewhere deep in my ribs – like old Stan hoping I can miraculously transform into a more heroic version of myself – I believe.

My short game's as lousy as any other part of my game, but occasionally I get lucky. I visualize a high floating lob that will land four feet from the hole, bounce minimally and roll within six inches. The shot I hit looks nothing like that. My backswing is balky and I jab at the ball and blade a one-hop line-drive that speeds toward the flag. If it misses hitting the pin it will skitter over the green and into the surrounding sand, but it doesn't miss the pin. Smacks it with a resounding clack and drops straight into the cup. The eagle has landed and we are eight under par after seven holes. At this rate, we will break the all-time tournament record. Gordon offers a hardy high-five but I suspect he's irritated. Lisa whistles and Natalie squeezes my shoulder and says, "Good aim, young man, superior aim." We skip lightly, all four of us laughing, to the next tee.

In the Flintmoor caddy tent, cheating was a much-discussed topic. Johnny Jones and other career guys advocated in favor of it. Johnny would say, "You gotta be sneaky. You want the members to play well. Lower scores mean higher tips and if they have a good round, they'll request you the next time. You can't let them know you're cheating for them though. It's only when they can't see you. It's only just if the ball's in the woods and stuck behind a tree in an unplayable lie, you just kick it a few feet so it's sitting in an open clearing with a shot at getting back to the fairway. Same thing in the high rough. If the lie's bad, nudge it a few inches so the shot's playable. The key is you don't just do it for the guys you're carrying for. You gotta do it for *all* the players in the foursome. That way everyone's happy. That way nobody complains about the supernatural luck everyone else seems to be having."

Gordon disagreed, though he never said so in the tent. He'd explain his theory to Lennie and me over spades games. "Look," he'd say. "These are guys who were living here, in America, during the Holocaust. They already feel like they cheated fate, like their whole life has been based on supernatural luck. What they want now is struggle. They want challenges to overcome, even bullshit ones like a golf ball behind a tree, because they survived Hitler without having to overcome anything. They've got relatives who were killed while they were over here eating pot roast with their mothers. Eating noodle pudding. The best thing you can do, when they're behind a tree, is to encourage them to take some crazy shot. Go for it, you gotta say, what've you got to lose? Listen, they'll probably miss the shot and then you can give that shrug that says, oh well, the whole world hates Jews anyway, and then you drop and take a stroke penalty and move on. But what if they hit the shot? What if they make that one miracle swing that makes them feel like Arnold Palmer? That's joy for them. In the middle of all this guilt they already live with, that's one hundred percent pure joy. It's the thing they search for when they come out here. They'll talk about that shot for the rest of their lives. Trust me, if they hit a shot like that, they'll tip you for days, maybe set you up with their nieces. Maybe sign over the papers to their Cadillac."

We're ten under par after nine holes. I haven't hit another good shot, not even close, but that doesn't matter. I don't need to. I have achieved my magical moment. We stop at the turn for a beer. Heineken. Lisa and Natalie quaff theirs in about twelve seconds and order another. "I think I'm in," Gordon says to me, nodding toward Lisa.

"She's dating another attorney," I say. "Good guy. Environmental law. Keeps our drinking water pure."

"He's not about to keep her pure, trust me."

When we finish the round, the four of us will sit in the clubhouse banquet room and be awarded a large trophy. We will also be awarded a case of aged scotch and various and sundry gift certificates. We will break open one of the bottles of scotch and relive the glories of our record-breaking day, especially my miracle chip shot on the seventh. Our in-firm band, The Sharks, comprised of oh-so-clever tort specialists who strum guitars and sing lyrics with smug puns about how smart we are and how stupid our clients, judges and jurors are, will play a twenty-five minute set and we will grow drunker and drunker and at some point I will realize it's just me and Natalie at the table, that Gordon and Lisa have slipped away to her BMW in the parking lot where he surely has two hands under her skirt. Natalie will look at me with slurred eyes and rivulets of scotch drool on her chin and say, "Hey, partner, care to demonstrate any more of your superior aim," and the sticky issue here, the high tangled rough, is that I'm already engaged.

Nancy Freiberg is not a lawyer and I'm not in love with her. Nor is she in love with me. We're both willing to settle. Physically, though she's not pretty, there's nothing obvious about her that's off-putting. She's a couple inches shorter than I am and she makes adequate money at her public relations firm and she sometimes smiles at the awkward comments I offer as jokes. I'd say we're compatible, but it's not even about that. We're tired of being alone, both of us. We intend to marry, buy a house with a cozy kitchen, present our best selves to the general public, and if we make it seven or eight non-miserable years together, we will have accomplished all we can hope for.

This is an appealing plan. I do not want to do anything to upset it. I'm all about the cozy kitchen, all about the parched forgettable sex. After today and my lucky eagle, I will be on the winning team. I will last another six months at the firm, possibly as much as two years if we break the scoring record, which will give me enough time to put out feelers for another job, and maybe Nancy and I will have children who will be smarter and more attractive than we are.

Still, I have never touched a woman as beautiful as Natalie.

More than most, I know how relationships can be spoiled by a single small temptation. I make my living off the hurt, the bitterness. I know – down to the last squirreled-away dollar – the cost of that kind of mistake.

Still, I have never touched a woman as beautiful as Natalie.

Nancy may not be a toasty oven-woman of a person, but she's honest. She's counting on me. We've set a date for next April and our parents are excited. They will help us with the down payment on our house. I have had fun today, no doubt, and a bit of luck, but there will not be any grand moments of defiance. I will not, literally or figuratively, throw any golf bags into a pond and strut blithely from the course of my life as if I'm some kind of fuck-it-all legend. I will not be ripping anything. I will be marrying Nancy and playing it safe.

Still, I have never touched a woman as beautiful as Natalie.

A few years ago I represented Gordon during his divorce. It was an easy job. The split was amicable and all Gordon wanted was to keep the health club membership in his name and to have Lenora put it in writing that she wouldn't work out there anymore. "If I'm gonna have to convince a whole new slate of women that I'm worth doing," he told me, "I have to get myself in shape. I can't be spending hours at the gym if she's there too, if she's trying to build herself a new body to share with other dudes."

Lenora saw the logic in that argument and the whole thing was settled in a trio of brisk two-hour meetings. "It's not that I don't love you, Gordon," she said to him as they left my office for the last time. "It's that I'm not sure I know how to love anyone. I'm not sure I even love myself."

Gordon described this assessment as both truth and bullshit. "What she's saying is true, but she has no understanding of it. She doesn't know how to love anyone, especially herself, and she has no clue about how to learn. She's just mouthing those words like the doctor told her to in therapy."

"What will you do now?" I asked him.

"I'll be me," he said. "I'll go to the gym. I'll make money. I'll lose more hair. I'll meet new women. I'll be all right."

Immediately after the divorce, we hung out quite a bit. Not at night when he presumably chased women – "I'm having success in that department," he'd tell me – but we'd meet twice a week for breakfast at a beat-up diner. "Best pancakes in the city," Gordon said. "Good coffee too. None of that tapioca-machiatto absurdity."

Once I asked him if he ever heard what happened to Newfeld and Bloch.

"Bloch died. Massive stroke. Newfeld's still alive. Stopped playing golf though. Ninety years old and still goes to the club to criticize the soup and terrorize the waitresses."

"How'd you ever make it through loops with those guys? How'd you survive that?"

"How you survive anything, man. How I survived Lenora. You just go inside yourself and think about something different. Think about how the world would be better if you had more control over it, how one day you will."

He went back to eating his pancakes. He didn't like to cut the whole stack and then spear large syrup-soaked chunks with his fork. Instead, he separated the pancakes like an Oreo cookie and chewed through them one layer at a time. What he was saying felt to me like truth, but with some bullshit mixed in too.

"That's all you did?" I said. "Just sucked it up and imagined a brighter day?"

He paused then, mid-chew, looked at me like he'd trusted me with the dissolution of his marriage and I'd managed to prove I was no longer a retard. Then he chuckled. "It's easier to ignore a couple of bitter bastards when you're not worried all the time about your hard-on."

I looked out the window, saw the beginning of snow, how it swirled over the black roof of the hardware store across the street like somebody was puffing soft, mint-flavored crystals.

"Actually, there's one other thing I used to do," he said. "You remember how Johnny Jones used to cheat for members and give them better lies?"

I nodded.

"I did the exact opposite. If Newfeld or Bloch hit into the woods and the ball was all right, like it was playable, I kicked it so it wasn't. I pushed it behind a tree or into a bush. The way I figured was if they were gonna be pissed off at the universe anyway, no matter how many breaks they got, why give them any breaks at all? Why not let every piece of evidence confirm their belief that every molecule in the world was out to get them? Fuckers."

This I know: I'm no hero. Not even a hero's sidekick. I'm a family lawyer specializing in amicable divorces. I get them done too fast and my firm leaks income. My teeth are straight now and my limbs are more proportional to my body, but I'm flabby and my nose is overlarge. I look exactly like no one worth trusting. Couples finalize their deals quickly because no one wants to spend time with me. Nancy, at least for now, claims she's willing to. She'll sit next to me and watch television. She'll say, "You're good at what you do, Bruce. Be proud."

When Nancy takes her clothes off, her skin is pale and, often, a bit cold to the touch. I'm obviously nothing special either. When our bodies move against each other, there are no fireworks. Still, we are kind to each other. I stroke the hair on the back of her neck and sometimes she cries. She tells me she's never let herself be vulnerable with anyone else. She trusts me because she knows I need someone to be vulnerable with too. We could be stuffed animals for each other, objects we'd like to grow out of but which, for now, we clutch onto with all we've got.

Inexplicably, it happens again on the sixteenth hole.

It's a short par four and after Lisa's rocket of a drive we are poised splendidly in the fairway, about eighty yards out. I go last this time. Gordon lobs a wedge to about ten feet. Good enough to let Lisa and Natalie fire dead at the flag. Natalie hits her worst shot of the day, a cut that lands in a flowerbed right of the green. "Sorry," she says. "Don't know what I was thinking."

I'm thinking maybe the beers are getting to her.

Lisa plays a bump-and-run that for a moment looks perfect, but it slows in a clump of grass and winds up about a foot outside of Gordon. "All right," Gordon says, as if there's no chance I'll hit anything closer. "Ten feet. One of us will knock it in."

I line my shot up and this time I do hit it just like I visualize. My backswing is smooth, the blade of my wedge digs a soft divot from the turf and the ball ascends in a gorgeous soaring arc. "That looks good," Lisa says and we all watch it, a miniscule dot against a sky that's swimming-lips blue. In our quiet, we can hear a cheer from a nearby hole. Some other group has made a birdie. Pathetic. Birdies are nothing to us. We are entitled to them. My ball lands half-a-foot from the cup, bounces once and drops into the hole. Another eagle. Lisa jumps high in the air with a shout and Gordon flips his wedge with an oh-my-fucking-god toss. Natalie scurries toward me on her toes and kisses my cheek, her mouth moist.

One day that caddying summer it was about ninety thousand degrees. The air was broth. I got sent out in a threesome with Gordon, all ladies who couldn't play to save their lives. They'd hit the ball twenty feet on the ground and then spend two minutes setting up and waggling and addressing the ball, and then hit it twenty feet again. The bag I was carrying was enormous and filled with golf balls and two umbrellas and even a sweater and an extra pair of shoes. The round was hot and endless and with three women and all that waggling, my boner was continuous and painful. In the middle of the fourteenth fairway, I was done. I couldn't carry that condominium of a bag one more foot and I dropped it a hundred-and-fifty yards from the green and sat down and hung my head. I couldn't have cared less if my bank account never grew another penny, I'd had it.

Gordon didn't hesitate. He walked over, scooped up the beastly trunk like it was somebody's mini change-purse and shouldered it. For the next hour-and-a-half, he carried all three bags, handed off clubs, and raked traps for all three women. All I did was pull pins. At the end of the round, practically in tears, I apologized to him. He called me a retard and told me to shut up. Then he gave me a third of his tips, the only tips I ever got. "Buy yourself some gum," he said. "Your breath stinks."

We are nineteen under par as we stride up the eighteenth

"You gonna come through for me?" Gordon asks me again. "Hold up your end?"

"Shut up," I tell him. "Your breath stinks."

I swing without paying much attention to what I'm doing. My arms are loose and flowing through contact and the click of club on ball is pure. It's another perfect shot. Every eye on the balcony zeroes in on it. The ravine sighs in resignation as the ball floats toward the flag. For a second, it looks like it might bounce and roll into the hole again for a third eagle, but nobody's that lucky. It scoots, then slows, and finally settles about four inches from the cup. A tap-in for birdie. The roar from the balcony is loud and long, the applause lasts for a minute at least.

I doff my hat and bow.

Natalie and I are in the basement of the clubhouse. In a small office that's empty except for a wastebasket with a handful of cough-drop wrappers and a greyish table pushed up against one wall. It's as if no one has decided yet what to use the office for. Natalie leans back against the table. I lean into her. Her golf shirt is on the floor and her bra is of a lace and smell that Nancy will never achieve in this lifetime. Gordon and Lisa disappeared an hour ago. "What would you do," I ask, "if in the middle of a round somewhere, your caddy gets so pissed off at you he throws your clubs into a pond?"

"That would never happen," Natalie says. "I treat my caddies well."

Her breath has been overwhelmed by the scotch. It is sweet and leafy, a summer forest at night, a bacchanalia. It is lush and fertile and way beyond the out-of-bounds marker and I think my tongue tastes the same way. Nancy would understand why I'm doing this, which will only make it hurt more when she finds out. I will lie to her, but I will also want to brag. It will be up to her to decide if she still wants to settle for me, and my lawyer's instincts tell me she will. It will not make her feel better when I tell her this is only a one-time deal, something special for me, kind of like a tip.

Yes, a tip is what this is. I performed well on the course and now I am being tipped.

I take Natalie's nipple into my mouth. It is alive. I am alive. Her stomach is a steam of fresh-baked bread, warm and gold and rising toward my cheek, my fingers. "Twenty under par," I say, as she unbuckles my belt.

Her hand holds me and demonstrates the authority of her grip. "This is not something we'll be telling the rest of the firm about," she says.

No, it isn't.

UNDER DANNY ROTTEN

Under this shirt is skin, and under this skin is heart, and under this heart, is nachos, my own full plate with diced jalapeños and the six of us – my two brothers, my sister, my parents and me – heading out to dinner in Mamaroneck on Saturday nights.

It was a twenty-minute drive, the inside of the station wagon warm, dark, fluid, a womb. We'd park for free on the street atop a hill a couple hundred yards from the restaurant, and walk down through a metered parking lot. Often, I held my mother's hand, or my little sister's thin fingers, but what burned was the anticipation of nachos. My own platter. And not a heaping mound of cheese-sauce and fake salsa slop, but a dozen individual chips, each with its own slather of freshly melted cheese, refried beans and a bold jalapeño in the center, juicy and staring, like an eyeball.

The back of the restaurant's menu taught me Mexican history I never learned in school, tales of Emiliano Zapata and Pancho Villa zooming across the countryside on horseback, shooting rifles and liberating farmers from the heel of fat and greedy landowners. Beneath the restaurant's faux stone arches, my parents would split a pitcher of Sangria, a quarter-chunk of lemon floating on the surface like a rowboat. A Mariachi trio circulated across the dining room's smooth ceramic floor and when the three men hovered near our table, my father slipped them a few dollars to play "Guantanamera."

No dining experience will ever compare to the ecstasy of that one, for years the only full meal I'd eat each week during wrestling season. My mouth would start to water sometime late Wednesday afternoon as I thought of the warm car-ride, the trek through the parking lot, and, at last, the restaurant's stiff high-backed chairs.

Then, minutes after we were seated, the hot metal platter would swoop over my left shoulder and land in front of me, sizzling.

It was always worth it, those nachos. That first tentative nibble of the cheese's soft goo, then the crisp of the chip's mildly resistant crunch, the combined flavor filling my mouth with an explosive surge. It was worth the grunt and sweat of a week eating little but lettuce, ice cubes, and raspberry jelly on whole wheat. It was worth the desperation that came with learning how to break down an opponent's base with a sharp arm-chop, knock the kid off-balance, and dig his shoulder and face – nose-forward – into the mat.

Under that desperation was Danny Rowton.

We called him Danny Rotten. He called himself that too, and bit the alligators off chests of preppy golf shirts worn by kids whose asses he could kick. Which was pretty much every kid who wore that kind of shirt. Which was pretty much why I never wore that kind of shirt. In front of a lunch-line of sixth graders, he once broke the arm of Timmy Anders – a semi-retarded kid – snapped it like a wish-bone, apparently for no other reason than he wanted to hear the sound it made when it splintered. Word had it that, at thirteen, he stole a car when he was drunk and crashed it through a police roadblock, killing a cop and shattering his own collarbone. Whether or not the story is true, it's why I joined wrestling. So I could learn how to apply pressure to Danny's already once broken collarbone and, if he ever tried to mess with me, crack that fucking thing all over again.

Under that fear was the paralyzing notion there were two sides of town, and I lived in the wrong one – the soft cheese one. The other side, where Danny lived, was Battle Hill, so named for the bravery of George Washington, who allegedly held the high ground there and beat the Redcoats back to their tea and crumpets. Perhaps in that tradition, perhaps because of its proximity to the train station, kids who lived on Battle Hill grew up tough and restless in cramped homes with well-worn rugs and the only television in the living room, the only telephone hanging on a wall in the kitchen. Kids from Ridgeway – my side of town – attended Hebrew school and played ping-pong in their spacious and finished basements. But not me.

Under our living room, the uncarpeted dampness held a light bulb without a fixture and a beat-up bench-press. I calloused my hands there, banging my head to AC-DC and Zeppelin, ten sets of ten every other day until no wimp-ass alligator shirt could contain my bulging pectorals. Shoulder-blades pushing into the bench's sweat-stinking vinyl, I shaped my vision around the bar cutting into my hands, a cold iron line that blocked my view of the ceiling. The only sight I could conjure as I breathed in and out through my reps, was Danny, hand over hand, scaling the rope in our middle school gymnasium, pulling himself all the way to the top where – incredibly – he held on with one hand, and with the other inked his name onto the support beam with a Sharpie.

He scrawled his name everywhere at that middle school – just the first name, Danny, in five aggressive capital letters, the Y at the end winding backward beneath the two Ns and terminating in a downward pointing arrow so it looked like the tail of the Devil. *Danny* on the backboards in the parking lot. *Danny* on the heating and cooling vents. *Danny* on the drinking fountains and bathroom stalls. *Danny* on the fire-alarm boxes and *Danny* on as many desks in as many classrooms as he could possibly inhabit. It was art and it was vandalism and it scared the shit out of the rest of us who believed Danny could be anywhere, at any time, ready to ink his name into your face with his fists and to add to his legend by kicking your ass.

He was fond of wearing a black t-shirt, emblazoned with the slogan "Death to Disco," a sentiment I could not understand back then, a year before AC-DC, Zeppelin and the bench-press. I was immersed in the gleeful throes of just discovering disco, celebrating the fun of its party-hard back-beats with an unconquerable ear-to-ear grin. I boogied down at Bar Mitzvah receptions, my penny-loafered feet spinning like propeller blades. My clip-on tie whipped back and forth with the crazed energy of a boy who knew Danny would never be invited to the Jewish kids' dance, and who also was beginning to understand that those bra-straps bumping out of the backs of the strapless dresses the girls wore portended something wondrous, some glorious hint of a future worth knowing.

Danny disappeared for a year after seventh grade, a vanishing that birthed the rumor of the stolen car, broken collarbone and dead cop. I spent the mysterious interval of his absence convinced he'd return any minute, feeling him like a ball of jagged teeth lurking in my head, ready to pounce and chomp on my chest. I discarded Donna Summer for Eric Clapton and pumped up in the basement, wanting to take full advantage of every moment Danny wasn't ubiquitous with his Sharpie. I got busy growing amusement-park dizzy on first kisses, and trembling a little too much to let my fingers do anything but graze the outside of the beckoning bra-straps.

Even now, I shiver thinking of it, the thrill.

At the onset of high school, Danny was back. Like me, he was beefier than before, none of it fat, and a scar that stretched across the front of his right hand looked like it could have been a knife-wound. We were assigned lockers in the same cul-de-sac, though I'm not sure why Danny needed one. He rarely carried books or wore a coat. Still, he checked in at his empty locker every day, opening and closing it with violence, turning to hiss at me: "Ross, you're a pussy."

I never said anything back, pretended I didn't hear and hoped Danny wouldn't decide to shove me, to cross over into the physical where I'd have to test my bench-pressed strength and the techniques I'd learned in wrestling practice. I could see my response developing, visualize it like golfers do before they hit their shots. He would lunge at me and I would grab his right wrist with both my hands, tie him up in a Russian two-on-one so I could leverage his head toward the ground. He would resist, trying to push back up, and I would use that momentum, rise with him so I could drive his wrist behind his back and fold it like a chicken wing. He'd react by jolting forward in an attempt to break my hold and when he jolted, I'd let go with my left hand and circle it around the top of his head, yanking his neck backward and – *pop* – there would go his collarbone, neatly split at its most vulnerable point.

It never came to that and I almost never wanted it to, until Danny stopped slamming his locker and used it instead as a surface he could slide his girlfriend against as he leaned in and sucked on her tongue. He was surprisingly tender toward her, holding her face with both hands as he kissed her, moving slow, talking quietly. I'd pretend to organize my textbooks, or to dig for homework, and watch them. I'd imagine she was a positive influence on him, would tame him enough to curb his desire to beat the piss out of me. When the warning bell sounded for first hour, he'd place an arm around her shoulder as if she'd break if his touch weren't light enough, and massage circles onto her back. Then he'd turn his head and mouth to me, "You're still a pussy, Ross. Always will be. A pussy supreme."

Whatever. I was used to ignoring his taunts. But I couldn't ignore his girlfriend, who was tender toward him as well, ruffling her fingers though his hair as they kissed, or slipping her hand into the back-pocket of his blue jeans as they walked. Danny Rotten's girlfriend was Caroline Haas, and I'd been in love with her since elementary school. Half-Filipina/half-Dutch, gorgeous. Athletic, she slid through the hallways like a dancer and starred for the cross-country team. Smart, she took all accelerated classes, labored through reams of homework, and earned a four-point. She had huge brown eyes, long dark hair that curtained across her forehead, soft round lips and a way of breathing that lifted her chest and made me want to bang my face against the corner of my locker-door until I drew blood. It was her bra-strap I'd always focused on most at the Bar Mitzvahs. I had no idea why she was dating Danny Rotten.

For the most part, upon reaching high school, he'd stopped writing his name everywhere. One morning though, I arrived at my locker to find it covered with his scrawl – a huge heart and several smaller ones surrounding it like satellites. Each was filled with his aggressive handwriting. *Danny loves Caroline. Danny loves Caroline.* All over my locker. I felt like I was staring at my tombstone. What had died was whatever sense of manhood I'd been trying to cling to. My pussification was complete.

That afternoon after class, as I stuffed my backpack with homework assignments it was doubtful I'd ever get to, and made ready to hustle down to wrestling practice, he showed up at the lockers, leering.

"Hey, king of all pussies," he said. "What're you doing? You want to come hang out with me and Caroline? I got beer."

"What do you mean?"

"I mean, dumbass, she's got a cousin from the city who wants to hang out. We need another dude to make shit even."

I didn't drink beer. The whole thing could have been a trap. Danny wanted to take me somewhere off school grounds so he could beat my ass without getting suspended. Plus, I had practice, and we had a match in a couple days against New Rochelle. But New Rochelle blew. It didn't matter who they'd try to run out there, it would be quick – forty-five seconds, a minute at most. Nothing fancy. Circle, shuffle, feint, shoot a double-leg takedown. Arm-chop to knock him from his base. A simple half-nelson to turn him over.

A simple half would do.

I looked at Danny. He was a devious fuck, but his face looked open, pleading. He had a serious problem. If he couldn't find another dude, his afternoon with his girlfriend might get ruined. Maybe he'd stop hassling me if I helped him out. Maybe Caroline's cousin would look like her. I threw my backpack into my tombstone locker and followed him.

We walked through the hallways and headed toward the gym area where the wrestling room was. I stayed behind Danny and kept my head down, hoping none of the coaches or any of my teammates would see me. We slipped out a side-door and Danny started jogging toward a tree-line about a half-mile away. "Hurry up, dude," he urged. "We gotta grab some food before they get there."

Outside was grey and about forty degrees, but I'd broken a sweat by the time we reached the woods. It made me feel loose and happy. Yeah, I was skipping practice, but I was getting some conditioning in anyway. We kept jogging in the woods on a small footpath I hadn't known existed and I was surprised at the kind of shape Danny was in. I knew he was strong, but I hadn't known he had endurance. He seemed hardly tired and I picked up the pace to see if he could keep up. "Good," he said. "Yeah. Let's move."

We ran faster. My lungs and legs were fine, but my stomach yowled in hunger. I hadn't eaten anything all day but a piece of dry toast for breakfast. The pangs worsened when the sound of automobile traffic linked itself to fumes bearing the telltale grease of a fast-food restaurant as we neared the edge of the woods. The path dumped us into a Burger King parking lot. We slanted past the drive-through line, slowed, and walked in. "I'm gonna get Caroline and Alisa some burgers and fries," Danny said, holding the door open for me. "What about you? Want anything?"

It was strange, this kindness. Maybe he knew there was no way I could eat anything like that and maintain my weight. I shook my head and tried not to breathe, not to smell anything as he stood on line and then ordered, but I couldn't take it, felt the words pushing toward my teeth to say *hey, on second thought, I'll have a milkshake, vanilla,* so I slinked outside to wait. He emerged after a few moments with a couple of bags and handed me one to carry before starting to jog back toward the woods. "Wait," I said, angling a thumb toward the market across the road. "I thought you said you had beer, or were getting it, or something like that."

"I do, dumbass, don't worry."

Again I followed Danny Rotten into the forest – each of us holding a paper bag of steaming burgers and fries – and this time, after we'd jogged a few minutes back on the path toward school, he veered left onto another trail I hadn't known existed. Who *was* he? Freakin' Ranger Rick? A couple minutes later, he turned and spoke. Finally, his breath seemed uneven. "Caroline would be kicking our ass right now," he said. "Girl can run forever. She's a fucking mutant."

I nodded because, yeah, she was a mutant, but not because of her running. Because she was beautiful and smart, and yet somehow attracted to this idiot. At least I knew how he got into the shape he was in, and how he knew how to navigate the forest. Clearly, he'd been running with Caroline, and these trails must be where her team trained. That depressed me for some reason – the two of them running together – as if their relationship might be deeper than just making out by my locker.

A few more minutes and we were out of the woods, this time opposite a chain-link fence I recognized immediately. It was the out-of-bounds barrier behind the fifteenth green at Flintmoor, my parents' country club. I'd played the hole dozens of times, and caddied it dozens more, but I didn't say anything when Danny led me to an opening in the fence, shushing me as he peeked through to see if any nutcase members were out in the fairway, braving the cold. It felt moronic to sneak onto property I could've walked onto through the front door, but there was no way I was going to mention that to someone known for biting alligators off golf shirts.

Nobody was around – "no Jewbags," Danny said – so we strolled boldly across the green and a couple hundred yards down the middle of the fairway, before cutting into the rough. Next, we headed toward a grove of trees that I knew hid a pond notorious for swallowing wayward slices from the tee-box. We trammeled through a layer of brush and then Danny led me on yet another thin trail, deeper into the woods and around to the back of the pond where I was stunned to see what looked like the ruins of an old stone house. Part of it had sunk into the brack at the pond's edge, leaving a roof that looked like a mound of dirt about six feet off the ground. We clambered up easily, put our Burger King bags to the side, and sat looking over the water. "It's from the revolutionary war," Danny said. "Soldiers hid supplies."

"No shit?"

"Yeah, man, you gotta know about stuff like this. Chicks love these fuckin' places."

The smell of the fries overwhelmed me. Probably they were emitting a last steam of warmth before beginning to cool, like a pheromone. I felt like grabbing both bags, ripping them open with my teeth, and scarfing. *Nachos,* I chanted to myself. *Just a few more days until the weekend. Hold out for the nachos.* Then I wondered, after skipping practice, if I even deserved them.

"I'm gonna get the beer," Danny said, and rolled off the side of the roof, jumping to the ground. I watched him push up the sleeves of his sweatshirt and scramble to where a half-submerged log poked a branch out of the pond. With one foot on the bank, he stretched his other across to stand on the log, reached down to hold onto the branch and steady himself and, then, balanced precariously, dipped his other hand into the water and pulled out a six-pack of Budweiser, the cans attached to each other with plastic rings. It was an astounding feat of athleticism, and I began to doubt the wisdom of my busting-his-collarbone battle plan.

He ducked inside the house on his way back up and ascended to the roof with the six in one hand and what looked like a ratty horse blanket in the other. "I steal these from a snack-bar over there," he said of the beer, pointing in the direction of the halfway house between the tenth and eleventh holes. "And this is for fucking."

He unfolded the blanket and spread it next to him. "I fuck

Caroline a lot here," he said. "I mean, so many times. She's good too. Alisa, yeah, you'll get something off her. She probably won't do you. Not on the first date. But you'll get something. You can watch us though. You like that, don't you? Watching me and Caroline?"

There were stones on the roof. I grabbed one and threw it deep into the water. Heard the clunk. Watched the ripples. No matter what, I could always throw.

"Nah, man," I said. "That's sick."

"Are you a faggot, dude? Seriously. 'Cause you're, like, ripped as hell. I mean, you look like you could bench a Buick, but I never see you with any females."

It was a legitimate question, one I can't say I hadn't asked myself. I'd loved dancing to disco, after all, but hadn't been laid yet. It was as if I'd loved the dancing just *for* the dancing. I hadn't treated it as a prelude to anything else. Too afraid to venture inside a bra, I hadn't even made a serious attempt to get laid. There was the wrestling thing too. All the rolling around with other boys. Tight singlets. Group showers.

"You want to touch it?" Danny said. "I'll pull it out right now. I don't give a fuck. Friction is friction."

I wondered if the girls were going to show up. If Alisa even existed. I threw another rock into the pond. Stood up.

"We can do this right here," I said. "You think you can kick my ass? Let's go."

Danny stood up too, a little annoyed it seemed, as if he had to handle an unpleasant task he'd rather have someone else deal with. He cricked his neck one time from side to side, then flexed. His forearms were taut and he was light on his feet, toes balled against the dirt roof. It felt then like the house had not been built for soldiers, but for us, for the tall leafless trees to ring us under the grey sky, right here, where he'd fucked Caroline Haas so many times.

I was calm though. Maybe I was about to get my ass kicked,

but maybe I wasn't. Either way, I could no longer be called a pussy. I circled and focused on his hands, watching to see which wrist I could grab and twist.

"Dude, chill," Danny said. "This ain't no WWF. I was just fucking with you. Have a beer."

I took one. I didn't like beer, still don't, and I knew the empty calories would mean twenty more minutes of conditioning. That didn't matter. There was no way I wasn't going to hit the basement bench for hours that night anyway, and there was no way I was going to turn down that beer.

We drank and I asked him why he didn't write his name everywhere any more, only on my locker. "In middle school, you want everyone to know you," he said. "In high school, it's like, fuck it, leave my ass alone. I got shit to do."

The sound of the girls' voices – their clatter through the woods – it felt like a miracle. Or maybe a disappointment. "That's so sweet," Caroline said to both of us, when she saw the fast food.

Alisa wasn't as pretty as her cousin, but Danny was right, she would give me something. Or, more like – huddled in a sand-trap, far from Danny and Caroline – she would offer, and I would take. More than I ever had before.

Back in school, Danny was cool with me after that. He stopped hanging out at our lockers, and never asked me to chill with him and any other girls, but he didn't mess with me either. Every once in a while – at a chance encounter in the hallway – he'd offer a nod of respect toward the accumulating number of safety pins on the sleeve of my wrestling jacket. Once, when we were seniors, and long after I already knew what college I was headed to, he asked if I'd help him study for the SATs. I said I would, but he never followed up, and it never happened.

Caroline went on to med school and married an orthodox Jew. I don't know what happened to Danny Rotten. Maybe he got married too. Maybe he's fat and happy and sells carpets. Maybe he has kids who steal cars and break into snack-bars. Maybe he's dead, or in prison. Maybe he leads wilderness trips for at-risk teenagers, and hasn't eaten a french fry in years.

The only thing I know for sure is his name's still on top of the gymnasium, black ink staring into history, devil-tail "Y" pointing to the floor. And under that, is me, the middle school wrestling coach, looking up, hungry, wondering if I can still react quickly to a whistle, chop an arm, break another kid down.

CAPTAIN AMERICA

In fifth grade, Eric Findley wanted a friend. We wanted to be superheroes, and we wanted a movie about superheroes. Specifically, we wanted a movie starring us as superheroes. Marvel only, of course, none of those DC losers like Batman or Superman or Green Lantern. What kind of wimpy crimefighter needs a lantern? Ooh, let me illuminate the villains with my green ray of light? Please. Take that thing on a camping trip and scare some mosquitoes, all right?

I was going to be Captain America. Adam Beneroff would be Mr. Fantastic, our brainiac leader. Benji Davis, a redhead, the Human Torch. Hilary Smith, the prettiest girl in the fifth grade, would be the Invisible Girl. She didn't know she would be the Invisible Girl. In fact, to her, it was we who were invisible. But that didn't matter. The thing was, if she were going to be invisible, she didn't actually have to be in the movie. We could just pretend she was on the set. No one would see her anyway.

Eric wanted to be Daredevil, the coolest superhero of them all. Blind fearless ass-kicker. It was understandable why Eric wanted to be blind. He was the ugliest kid we knew. He rarely showered and dandruff and grease stuck to his hair in tapioca-like clumps. The acne on his face was urban sprawl. His teeth were straight but filthy, caked with a cheese-colored gunk. His breath stank always of Doritos. We imagined his mother in the supermarket pushing several carts full of economy-sized bags of them, their crinkly foil announcing her arrival at the cash register with a continuous cracking sound, like ice breaking on a not-frozen-enough lake.

Eric was pudgy too, and not very tall; and we didn't want him in the movie.

We practiced karate-kicks during recess and back-flips off the monkey bars, landing on our feet ready to slash our fists at whichever overconfident evildoer smugly thought we'd already been vanquished. This, we knew, was the essential weakness of villains. They underestimated the good guys, always believed we were finished when we weren't. All we had to do was dig into our unlimited stores of courage and heart, replenish our battered muscles with the fuel of our fundamental goodness and wipe the cocksure grins off their collective wily faces. We were always one karate kick away from beating ass. Eric, never a karate kick away from anything but an infected zit, stood off to the side watching, occasionally shadow-punching the air around him, or walking on the ground-level balance beam and closing his eyes to practice being blind.

"My uncle's a Hollywood producer," he told us. "I wrote a script and sent it to him. He said he might be interested."

"That's bullshit," Adam said. "Your uncle's a loser, like you."

There was logic in that assessment, biological certainty, yet somewhere in us, we clutched at the dream. What if Eric really did have an uncle in Hollywood? What if he had written a script?

Eric was horrid, but he could write. We'd all seen Hilary Smith look up from her perpetual note-passing to Tricia Foster – the second prettiest girl in the fifth grade – when, in Language Arts, Eric read his story aloud about a lonely grasshopper. We thought it was embarrassing, how the bug's legs sawed a plaintive tune that made the attendant blades of grass sway with melancholy. It was disgusting, putrid in every sense, but Hilary had reclined her head against the rim of her chair, her waterfall of blond hair splashing on the windowsill behind her as she gazed dreamily upward at a cluster of pencils stuck in the ceiling. We would never forget how her mouth opened slightly, how her lips pursed as her fingers spread out long and slender on the skin of her jeans under her desk. Perhaps she thought her hands beneath the desk were invisible, but to us they were glowing, as if Eric's story had transformed her from the undetectable Susan Storm into Jean Grey, the fiery Phoenix, an aura of flame rising from her skin, and we were the ones bathing in her heat.

Every time we back-flipped off the monkey bars, the girl we were saving from certain death as she plunged off a collapsing bridge was Hilary Smith. Every time we aimed our karate kicks into the air, we were going for the throat of the heinous villain who held a shotgun to Hilary's cheek and threatened to blow her beautiful mouth into the tennis courts. Of course, if Hilary were home sick, our kicks were trying to save Tricia Foster. If both of them were home sick, then we were split on who should play the Invisible Girl.

Adam felt that Karen Watson, a Japanese girl who'd been adopted by an American family and basically raised white, was the next prettiest prospect. While we all agreed she was talented at being invisible, Benji argued that another Karen, Karen Hitchcock, who wore her hair exactly the way Hilary did, was prettier. While Karen Watson was definitely cute, he insisted her parents' whitening left her in a perpetual state of confusion. We'd often notice her trying to catch her reflection in a windowpane as she picked at the wings of the horrible Farrah Fawcett blowback her parents made her wear and tried to imagine what she'd look like if she could just comb it naturally straight. We tried to imagine that too, but reiterated to Benji that if Karen Watson were invisible, it wouldn't matter what her hair looked like. Benji countered that Karen's invisibility was irrelevant. We were superheroes. We'd be able to sense her confusion. Then, in a tight scrap, we wouldn't be able to trust her. A smart villain could exploit that weakness.

If Eric had an opinion about which girl we should try to save when both Hilary and Tricia were sick, he never offered it. Or if he did, we never cared enough to listen. I sided with Adam and we won the argument when I pointed out that if Tricia were absent and Hilary weren't, then Hilary would pass notes to Karen

Watson. "That must say something," I said. "Hilary clearly knows who's pretty, because she's pretty. She's the expert."

Benji was probably right when he said Hilary preferred Karen Watson only because she didn't like how Karen Hitchcock tried to imitate her hairstyle, but Adam ended the debate when he said, "Who made *you* the expert on hair, Flamebrain?" causing Benji to be self-conscious about his own unruly crop, and to stand next to Karen Watson at the windowpane tugging despondently at the ends of his floppy orange curls.

We were all big on rankings in that school. We ranked the girls, who ranked us, or maybe not us, but probably other boys. The teachers ranked everyone. It was their consensus that Eric Findley was not only the best writer in the fifth grade, but also better than any writer in the sixth grade. Adam and I agreed that was bullshit too, not so much Eric being better than the older kids – we also thought the older kids were lame, nearly lame enough to be DC superheroes – but we disagreed that Eric was a better writer than me.

I'd already, after all, sent half-a-dozen story proposals to the immortal Stan Lee at Marvel. Most of them centered around Captain America battling the Red Skull on a submarine deep in the North Atlantic, or Daredevil waging war against the Kingpin in Hell's Kitchen. I thought fighting sequences were my biggest strength. I could always write the heroes into a place where it seemed like the villains were about to win, and then, somehow, Cap or DD would dig into those limitless reserves of heart and courage and throw the perfect elbow jab to save the day. All my proposals got rejected, but on one of them – a strange effort where Captain America actually lost a battle to the Red Skull and wound up floating on his shield in the middle of the Atlantic, barely alive, beaten and depressed, wondering if good could ever truly triumph over evil – a guy who signed his name *Morris Balmer, Intern,* wrote a short personal note on the form letter. "Not bad, Lawrence," the note said. "Keep at it."

Adam was excited when I showed it to him. "See," he said, "this proves the shitbrain teachers don't know what they're talking about. You're definitely a better writer than Eric."

"The letter's cool," Benji said, "but don't forget what Eric did with his grasshopper story."

We hadn't. Benji's reminder made all three of us pause for a second and envision Hilary as she ceased her note-passing and contemplated the pencils in the ceiling, how she lolled her head back and stretched her fingers against her thighs.

"What if Eric really does have an uncle in Hollywood?" Benji said. "What if he did write a script?"

Two days later Benji told us he was going out with Karen Watson. He said it when he was sitting in a heap on the ground, his lanky legs clumped over each other like dirty laundry. He'd fallen off the monkey bars and twisted his ankle. "I'm distracted," he said. "I don't know if I can be The Torch anymore."

"What are you distracted by?" I asked him.

"I have a girlfriend now," he said. "Karen Watson. That's a weakness. A smart villain could kidnap her to get to me. I'm vulnerable."

"Bullshit," Adam said. Even though we agreed Karen was, at best, the third prettiest girl in our class, still, she was way too pretty for Benji.

"I'm serious," he said. "You know how I sometimes stand next to her at the windowpane?"

"Of course, moron, *you're* not invisible," Adam said.

"Yeah, well," Benji said, "this morning when I was standing next to Karen, she said she could sense I was a nice person. So I asked her out. Watch, I bet she sends Hilary a note in class to tell her about it. I bet Hilary reads the note."

Perhaps Adam could already sense that Benji didn't really have the heart to fight evil, that in three weeks he wouldn't bother coming to the Marvel Comics convention in Manhattan, that in four weeks he'd barely talk to us at all. Maybe that's what made Adam so angry at Eric.

For a long moment, he looked over at the four-square court where the girls – Hilary, Tricia and the Karens – gathered to talk, not even to hold a ball, not even to play anything. Then he stomped one foot against the dirt and seemed to gather a sense of purpose in his chin.

"It's time," he said, his words slow and determined. "Time for us to find out if that loser's been lying to us."

We marched the thirty feet from monkey bars to balance beam in a three-pronged wedge, Adam at the lead. It was our first mission and we could feel our reserves of courage burning our chests. Even Benji seemed to perk up. After months of back-flipping and karate kicks, we were itching to be heroes. Itching for truth.

That Eric, as he plodded along the balance beam with his eyes closed, failed to hear us approach, was further proof he'd never cut it as Daredevil. "Hey, Fuckbrain!" Adam shouted and then shoved him roughly, knocking him off the six-inch high beam.

To Eric's credit, he landed on his feet, though in an awkward half-crouch, hardly an effective fighting stance.

"Where's the script, Fuckbrain?" Adam asked him.

"I told you," Eric said, "I gave it to my uncle. He said he had to show it around to people. And it's not a script anyway. It's a *treatment*, a proposal for an idea to write a script about."

"Treatment" seemed to slow Adam down for a few seconds. It sounded like the kind of authentic term people in Hollywood might actually use, and it felt similar to the Marvel process. First, you had to sell the idea to the people in charge, then you had to write it.

"You are so full of shit," Adam finally said. "I should kick your ass right now."

"No," Eric insisted, practically crying. "I'm not lying, I swear."

He shook his head then, forcefully, as if he too were trying to summon some inner store of heart and courage. The net effect though, canceling out his repeated pleas that he was telling the truth, was that a nugget of grease-glued dandruff about the size of a piece of popcorn dislodged itself from his hair and fell to the ground. A flurry of ants scrambled immediately to eat it.

"My God," Adam said. "That's the most disgusting thing I've ever seen."

It looked for a moment like Adam was about to kick Eric's ass right there, like he'd punch his puss-filled face. Instead, he smiled. It was an overconfident villain smile, a leer. "You guys wait here," he said to Benji and me. "Keep an eye on the loser. Don't let him run."

Of course, Eric wasn't going to run. He could barely stop his potato-sack body from shaking. Still, Benji and I had been charged with our first assignment. We were alert. We took our jobs seriously. "If you run, you're dead," I said, crossing my arms like a sentinel.

Adam was gone less than a minute, the amount of time it took him to march back to the monkey bars and retrieve his Incredible Hulk lunchbox. He opened it and pulled out the plastic bag of carrots his mom had packed for him, then dumped the carrots on the ground, not far from Eric's distressing dandruff clump. The ants failed to react to the appearance of the carrots. Apparently, to them, the dandruff clump wasn't ugly at all. They would've ranked it highly.

Adam turned the plastic bag inside out and shoved his hand inside it, then, in the manner dog-owners use to clean up after their pets, he bagged Eric's chunk of popcorn-dandruff, sweeping up a huddle of ants with it and then pulling his hand out and sealing the zip-lock top. I wondered if the ants would be able to breathe.

Do ants breathe?

"All right, Fuckbrain, I'm not gonna kick your ass now," Adam said to Eric. "You've got one week to prove you're not lying about your uncle. One week. If you can't prove it by then, not only will

I kick your ass, but I will make you eat this disgusting shit too."

Adam put the baggie with Eric's dandruff greaseball into his Hulk lunchbox. I wondered if he'd keep it there for the whole week, if he'd be able to eat anything forced to share space with it, if he'd ever again eat anything, a single thing that came out of that lunchbox.

That was the last time Benji hung out with us during recess. The next day he sat on a picnic table on the other side of the playground with Karen Watson. They didn't hold hands, but they sat close to each other, legs touching. That's when Adam got the idea I should go over to Eric's house and co-write the script with him.

"But he already wrote it," I said.

"He just wrote a treatment," Adam said. "Plus, this way you can scout around and see if it's bullshit about his uncle."

I wondered why Adam couldn't scout around Eric's house. He was sneakier than I was. I wasn't much of a sneak at all, which was probably why Captain America ranked so high on my list of heroes. He wasn't sneaky either. Just tough. Full of heart. Full of integrity. Still, I wasn't going to argue the point with Adam. If he thought I was the best man for the job, I would accept the mission.

I couldn't help feeling a little pissed off a couple afternoons later, after school, when Eric led me into his house. It had to be a rare occurrence, his having a friend over, yet he seemed hardly excited. "Want a snack or something?" he said, as if offering in order to be polite, as if he actually preferred me to starve.

I expected the kitchen to be filled with Doritos, but I didn't see a single bag, couldn't detect a hint of the fake cheese scent. There were a dozen boxes of Malomars in a large closet though, which Eric called a pantry. "Take as many as you want," Eric said.

I loved Malomars. I opened one of the boxes and took six. "That's a lot," Eric said. "Don't take any more."

We trooped down to the basement – Eric called it the playroom

– which was finished and had a furry brown rug. I trembled to think what critters from Eric's hair might have fallen into that rug and nestled there without ants to eat them, or Adam to scoop them up with sandwich bags. I sat in a leather recliner and pulled my feet off the floor. There were twenty or so plastic swords and several suits of fake armor scattered around and I wondered whom Eric played with in the playroom.

In a corner, beneath a poster of Daredevil mugging with his billy club as if he were about to crack somebody's forehead, a large plastic bottle, nearly four feet tall, was more than half-filled with change. There had to be thousands of pennies and several hundred nickels, dimes, and quarters. "Damn," I said. "How much money is that?"

"I don't know," Eric said. "My mom started it when I was little. Every time we go out, we come back and dump our change in there. She wants it to be my college fund."

I realized I could beat Eric's ass and steal it. It would be heavy to carry, but I'd gotten strong from all the back-flipping and air-punching. I could buy a lot of cool stuff with that money, maybe enough to impress Hilary Smith, or Tricia Foster. I was too afraid to do it though.

Maybe Daredevil scared me.

"What about your dad?" I said. "Does he put change in there too?"

"I don't know anything about my father," Eric said. "Not one thing."

It occurred to me then that maybe his story about the pathetic grasshopper had been less about his standing off to the side of Adam, Benji, and me, pretending we liked him when we didn't, and more about his having fake swordfights with his invisible father in his basement. "Who plays with all this stuff?" I asked.

"Mostly me. I pretend I'm different characters. I have some cousins in New Jersey. Sometimes they come here."

I was quiet, watching him. Pitying, I guess. Who wants to play with people from New Jersey? Everyone has cousins there, though. That's the kind of state it is. A lot of traffic on the parkway.

Suddenly, Eric got excited, more animated than he'd been all afternoon. "Hey," he said, gesturing at the swords and shields. "Do you want to –?"

There was no way I was going to play with Eric's bullshit swords. "Maybe later," I said. "Let's work on the script and see how much time we have."

We heard a noise upstairs, someone entering the house. "My mother," Eric said.

She clattered around in the kitchen for a bit, putting bags of the missing Doritos into the pantry, I assumed. Then we heard her call downstairs. "Eric?"

"Down here," he said. "In the playroom."

Where else would we be? The boiler room? The kid disgusted me. His mom came down the stairs. Her heels made a knocking sound and from where I was sitting on the recliner, they were the first things I saw. Then legs. Muscular calves and the lower parts of thighs until they disappeared beneath the hem of a black business skirt. A thin waist was next, with a tucked-in blouse that tightened around breasts that looked like mountains.

I was in fifth grade. I knew nothing about breasts. Nothing about mountains. Still, even before her neck and face descended into view, I knew she was going to be more beautiful than Hilary Smith. A lot more beautiful.

Her hair was dark and thick like Eric's, but not greasy. No dandruff. She was tall and athletic-looking, and she reminded me of Linda Carter, who played Wonder Woman on TV. Wonder Woman was a DC superhero, so Adam, Benji and I all had to agree she was a joke. But the truth was Wonder Woman was much less a joke than the Invisible Girl. We could see Wonder Woman. We watched her series every week. Her bracelets that were supposed to stop bullets, those were garbage, everybody knew that; but those immense legs thrust forward like *pow*, that low-cut golden bustier in your face like *bam* – all that skin – there was definitely something superheroic going on when she stood tall in a dark alley, arms akimbo, daring evildoers to make their move.

Eric's mother seemed startled to find someone beside her son in the playroom, but she recovered quickly and extended her hand. "I'm Eric's mother," she said. "Nice to meet you."

Her hand was warm, but not in a gross sweaty way, and I could think of nothing to say, and anyway Daredevil was glaring at me, so I didn't say anything.

"This is Lawrence, from school," Eric said. "He's gonna be Captain America."

Eric's mother had nothing to say to that, didn't smile, kind of half-glanced at me as if she didn't really believe I had the stuff to be a crimefighter with integrity. A crimefighter with heart. Instead of talking more, she leaned down and kissed her son – twice – once on the disgusting nest of his hair, and then smack in the middle of the acne morass on his chin. Neither time did she flinch. It was as if nothing about her son disgusted her *at all*. She pulled a handful of change from her purse and dumped it in the big bottle. "Are you boys thirsty?" she said. "I'll bring you down some sodas."

But she never did, and that was the last I saw of her before I left the house. Eric and I forgot about the sodas too, once we began to work on the script. At first, we wrote separately, me on the recliner, he lying on his elbows on the disgusting rug. "Read aloud what you have so far," he said after fifteen minutes.

I started in on one of my scenes with Captain America and the Red Skull going at it in a submarine, and read to the point where Cap throws his shield and severs one of the Skull's arms. "Cool," Eric said, in the same I'm-just-trying-to-be-polite way he offered me Malomars. "Check out what I got."

The story that unfolded was riveting. Daredevil and Captain America were teamed up against Doctor Octopus, who'd already kidnapped Spiderman and drugged him into submission. Octopus proposes a trade. You can have Spiderman back, he says, if you both surrender. Spiderman, Dock Ock argues, saves more lives than both of you combined. He's more powerful. I'll let him walk free to do all that good work, save all those lives, as long as you two agree to be my prisoners.

It was a horrible equation. It made me wonder what I'd do if I had a choice to go out with either Hilary Smith or both Tricia Foster and Benji's so-called girlfriend Karen Watson. In Eric's version, Daredevil wants to make the deal but Captain America doesn't. "I may not save as many people as Spidey," Captain America says, "but I'm a national symbol. I stand for something."

"I don't know about this," I said. "Captain America seems too scared, like he's wimpy."

"But that's what makes it interesting," Eric whined. "If the hero always does the right thing, it's boring. If the hero always wins, it's too predictable."

I knew he was right. The note from Morris Balmer, Intern, which said "Not bad, Lawrence," when I wrote about Cap floating half-dead on his shield, proved his theory. Still, did I really want to play a weasely Captain America?

"Listen," I said, to change the subject. "Doctor Octopus seems like he'd be a really complicated costume with those titanium tentacles. I mean, we're gonna have costumes, right? Like your uncle's gonna hook us up with some really cool costumes?"

"Well, yeah, I guess so, if he likes the script. Yeah, sure we'll have costumes. Not the Invisible Girl, of course."

"Right, because she won't need a costume."

"Right, because no one will see her."

Maybe it was the realization Eric actually was a better writer than I was that made me say what I said next. Maybe it was the recognition that Hilary Smith and the shitbrained teachers knew the truth.

I heard his mother clattering some more above us, and I wanted her to come down again, but I knew she wouldn't.

"Maybe your uncle can give you, like, a sample or something," I said. "Before the week's over, just, like, part of a costume. Then you can use it as proof so Adam won't kick your ass."

Eric looked doubtful. I glanced at his plastic swords and made a slashing motion with my hand as if I were actually thinking about playing with him, actually thinking about pretending to be some kind of character. "I don't know," he said. "Yeah, okay, maybe."

That maybe was all I needed.

"Eric says he'll have part of a costume for us before the deadline," I told Adam the next day. "That's what he said the proof will be."

"You'd better not be lying, Fuckbrain," Adam said to Eric when he found him shadowboxing by the balance-beam.

"If you don't have something to show us by Monday, you know what you'll be eating," he added, pointing to his Incredible Hulk lunchbox.

The weekend plowed by in relentless fashion, faster than I wanted it to, like that evil mutant The Juggernaut who busted through any wall in front of him and just kept moving. I wanted The Mighty Thor to ring the heavens with his hammer and create a storm violent enough to wash away the next week of school. I wanted Dr. Doom to poison the water supply to Eric's house so he'd be out sick a few days and Adam would forget the whole thing, or at least decide who was next in the rankings to be threatened, even if that turned out to be me. I wanted Eric's father to return triumphantly from where Mephisto had imprisoned him in an underground cave, wanted him to clutch his son in his burly arms and speed him away to California so we'd never see him again. I thought about Eric's mom a lot too, especially after watching Wonder Woman on TV on Sunday night.

I stayed up late after that, doing push-ups in the family room until my arms felt like flag-poles.

Unfortunately, Eric showed up on Monday. Before he opened his backpack, he warned us. "Remember," he said, "this is just a prototype. A model. It's not what the real costume will look like."

"It better be good, Fuckbrain," Adam said.

It was the saddest thing I'd ever seen.

It was navy blue and in the shape of a ski mask, the kind bank-robbers wear, with two uneven cut-outs for eyes, except it wasn't a ski mask. It was made from stretchable material, not wool. Some kind of nylon. Maybe it was two pantyhose knitted together. Two triangles, white ones, were sewn to the sides. They looked like mouse-ears. Stuck to the forehead region with a safety pin was a piece of a white pillowcase, cut into the shape of a star. "What is it?" I asked, but I already knew.

"Well, remember, it's just a prototype," Eric said, "but this is Captain America's cowl."

"This is such bullshit," Adam said. "Captain America's mask is light blue, like ocean blue, not navy blue. And he has wings on it, Fuckbrain, not panda ears."

Later I would wonder why Eric chose my superhero to try and create a costume-part for, and not a Daredevil billy club for himself, or even a stretchable glove for Adam. Maybe it was because for five minutes I'd swung plastic swords with him in his playroom. Maybe he thought I wouldn't betray him.

While Adam was bashing Eric's head against the tennis court fence and prying open his mouth so he could force him to swallow the dandruff ball and accompanying dead ants, I didn't think about any of that. All it would have taken to stop Adam was one spinning kick to his chest. A well-placed karate chop to the back of his head. Instead, I looked over to the picnic table where Benji was absorbed with Karen Watson and a few feet away, where Hilary Smith stood, staring.

I pictured Eric's mother staying up late to sew the cowl – stitching maybe at the exact same time I was doing push-ups – how she must've grown too tired to do the star, how Eric was left to pin it on by himself. Maybe the pantyhose were hers. I decided that no matter what happened, I wanted that cowl. Wanted to press it between my fingertips. No matter what happened, I wanted, at least once, to wear that cowl on my face.

MYLAR MAN

The Mylar Man claws through the sand. His fingers dig and tug bits of balloon and balloon-ribbon and I walk next to him because the Mylar Man is my brother and I love the Mylar Man. But more than that, I love his wife.

I'm a lousy brother. That's not debatable. Yet, I'm walking next to the Mylar Man and most people are afraid of the Mylar Man because his back and shoulders have grown knotty and hunched from crouching and digging, and his fingertips are raw and dark and flaking. Only I call him the Mylar Man. No one else, except for his wife – except for Naomi – even talks to him. She calls him Warren, which is his name, and he calls himself Old Goat on his blog *The Human Factor* where he writes daily about the ravaging and pillaging of the environment. He lives in a slowly deteriorating house on a bluff on the southeast shore of Lake Michigan and he is not old, only forty-two.

Naomi's younger, my age, just thirty-seven, and she owns the house. It's been in her family for a hundred and nine years. Old Goat has no job and doesn't do anything except flail against humanity on his keyboard for several thousand words a day, and walk four miles on the beach after dinner in quest of balloon remnants.

He hates latex balloons, which is what he mostly finds. At least those eventually decompose, he tells me. Maybe it takes six months, then longer for the ribbons, and it's likely large numbers of birds and turtles die from eating them, but eventually they go back to the earth. Mylar balloons don't. They never decompose. They float in the water looking like giant tasty jellyfish, or they make their way to the beach and nestle in the sand. Then they live there, like hermits, dead but alive too, until the Mylar Man finds them, and bags them, and throws them in the trash.

"Look at this one," he says.

It's heart-shaped, but little of the paint that once adorned it remains, just a few white frills and splotches of red. "What does something like this have to do with love?" he says. "This is a symbol of non-love. This is symbol of violence. Profess your love to your girlfriend by buying one of these, and you're professing your hatred of your planet. This balloon is a death-sentence to your grandchildren."

"Don't aim your Old Goat venom in my direction," I say. "I didn't let it go."

"You would have though," he says. "If you had someone you were in love with, you'd do it. You're romantic and stupid. I know you."

He does know me. And I am stupid, though not romantic. I wouldn't give his wife a balloon on Valentine's Day, just an earth-shattering orgasm that would make her forget her planet entirely. Naomi is short, under five feet, and a fireball of thick brown hair and compact muscular body that I know will just shake and shake and I wonder if my sand-clawing brother has any clue how to make her happy. She always seems happy, always laments the state of her falling-down house with a fond joke. Says, "Don't sit on that side of the dining room, you might wind up bobbing in the lake," and when she jogs barefoot on the beach she travels far away from her husband digging up balloons. Her gait is forceful and resolute. I want to catch her behind one of the dunes and hold her around her shapely waist and whisper to the top of her lush, rain-forest head, "I will not let you support me with your job teaching kindergartners while I rant and rave to either no one or maybe just a small pathetic cadre of other on-line whack-jobs. Together, we can save each other and your family-home and keep it from falling into the surf."

Naomi is friendly to me, but wary. She knows what I'm after, has always known it. I ask her why she teaches kindergarten instead of high school, why she wouldn't want students who can challenge her intellectually, explore probing questions.

"Do you know what a Word Wall is?" she asks me.

I don't.

"My kids learn how to spell *is*. They lean how to spell *of* and *the* and *and*. They look at these words every day on a wall, the curves and lines and dots. They watch these words with their eyes and live inside them and spell them in the air with their fingers."

Naomi is stirring pasta salad when she tells me this. She discards the spoon and reaches into the bowl of cold risotto, kneading the mixture of grain and olive and tomato with her hands as if she's a sculptor working with clay. Her hair is tied behind her head in a tight ponytail.

"I've seen high school kids," she says. "They don't know what recess is. If you tell them to go outside and play, they'll pull their phones from their pockets and start texting. I'm a patient person. I get nervous when I see that."

I watch her play with the pasta. She pulls her hands out then holds up an index finger and licks it. Makes a puzzled face. Digs back into the pasta, points the finger toward me. "Taste this," she says."

I lean forward.

"No, don't," she says, pulling her finger back. "It needs salt."

"Look at this one," the Mylar Man says, after he's waded hip-deep into the water to retrieve a balloon that's still partially inflated, his cut-off jean-shorts now soaked. "From Chicago, I bet. Some idiot let it go during a festival. Ate too many chili-dogs and didn't give a shit about his grandchildren's future and just let it fly."

The mylar is a familiar design, once a glowing yellow moon-pie with a smiley face, like a floating LSD tab, with two black dots for eyes and a slice of semi-circle for a mouth. Most of the yellow paint is gone, but the smiley face remains, looking like a leer now, a grin, more taunting and scary when its background is transparent.

"I understand the impulse," the Mylar Man says. "It's fun to let go of things. To feel a sense of release when something you've been holding too long drifts away. Your load lightens. But here's the thing, John." He pauses for a moment to stare at me and he looks like a God, bronzed and unhunched, silhouetted by the sky's pink embers. He is beautiful, my brother, always has been, a force of skin and beard and purpose. "John," he says, "it's an illusion. Life is never carefree. If you don't care, you die."

I had a balloon exactly like this yellow one once, when I was after Rachel. She had an eight-year-old son named Micah, and I tried to fill my apartment with all manner of playthings like baseball cards and Hot Wheels cars and plastic machine-guns and balloons so he wouldn't mind when I spent significant time with his mother in the bedroom. Rachel dumped me for a guy who makes hinged models of teeth and sells them to dentist offices – Micah started a collection and likes to polish them to a sparkle with a toothbrush and shaving cream – and I don't know what happened to the big yellow balloon. It wasn't hard to let Rachel go. If she drifted to the clouds, growing smaller and smaller each time I looked until finally I could no longer find her in the sky – fair enough, happy flying. Land safely with the teeth-maker.

Chicago – the idiot city, my brother calls it – is where I live. Not exactly plunk in the wind-battered big-shouldered heart, but in a bleak condo-town on the outskirts. My apartment, where I used to encourage Micah to cultivate imaginary friends as I investigated his mother below the belt, is characterless. The pool and fitness center in the condo-town clubhouse are poorly maintained; embarrassing, I'd say, so when my Dad travels out of town, which he often does for his consulting job where he draws shapes and arrows on legal pads, I borrow his Lincoln Park brownstone and bring women there. Always nice to fuck people on the four-thousand dollar leather couch where, when he's not traveling, my father also fucks people while my mother is home sleeping with the over-sized hemp-filled penguin my dipshit older brother and I mistakenly bought her one Christmas so she wouldn't be lonely. She hates that stupid non-animal with its creepy glass eyes and bright orange beak. She hates all it mockingly represents, but she'll never tell that to the Mylar Man or to me because she wants us to believe we harbor a modicum of essential goodness, which neither of us actually do believe, but when we're home visiting, we're willing to fake it to make her happy.

That's the kind of family we have, but none of that bothered me if the woman I was screwing on my father's couch was attractive enough, or groaned audibly. Except that one night my father's phone rang while I had a mouthful of breast and when the machine came on, one of my father's many paramours left him a message that said, "Franklin, when you get back to town, call me. I owe you a back massage."

It's bad enough to hear the voice of my father's lover leave him a message while I'm trying to bang a woman I'm not in love with because she's not my brother's wife who I am in love with – who I've always been in love with since the first time I saw her running the 400-meter hurdles back in high school – but it's worse, way worse, when the message spews frothy cheese like *I owe you a back massage.* Face it, nobody wants to imagine his father as one half of a horny adolescent couple so ashamed of its desires it has to mask them with the pretense of backrubs. The squawking-bird voice embedding itself in my father's apartment left me spitting breast from my mouth and sitting rigid on the couch because I realized my dad caused my mother a quantity of misery so gargantuan I can hardly talk to her for fear of disappointing her with all I've never lived up to, and the thing is – is this what it was all for?

Some pathetic slitbag still playing the same act that probably worked twice, or maybe three times prior to the middle school pool party season when everyone started trying it and there was an outbreak of backrubs at every encounter between the sexes, and then, as rapidly as acne, the movement began to reek of its own self-conscious stink?

All of which is to say I'm sorry for forgetting the name of the woman whose nipple I spit out, and for walking her so quickly back to the dance club she had to hold her heels in one hand and half-jog to catch up with me, but the fact is when I heard the shrill and candied chirp of my father's lover, I finished up quick – one final and shameful spurt – and had to evacuate the brownstone immediately because I knew it was a wrong thing, a profanity against nature for Naomi to be with my brother when I loved her more than he did.

Here's one truth: my father, who at sixty-seven continues to dye his hair with a paste as thick as shoe-polish and wear a diamond stud in his left ear, is nevertheless heroic. He left my mother but on some level I understand it. She's needy and nerdy and has an ornithological proclivity to find out everything she can about penguins even if she doesn't like sleeping with a creepy stuffed one. He's a big strong guy with big strong hands and his voice is deep and musical enough to make people believe in the magic of his shapes and arrows and his laugh is the kind of laugh that restaurants refer to as ambiance.

Yet my mother, for all her faults, is a sturdy woman grounded in a kind of natural and beautiful earthiness. In that way, she's like Naomi: like the naked elemental world somehow pushed up from its mud and gave her the gift of understanding its primordial dance. I'm in love with that quality. It feels both rare and brimming with redemption, as if it offers a kind of daily rebirth. All of which is to say my mom is capable of much more than cheeseball massages. Much more truth and much more spirit and maybe my dad just got overwhelmed and couldn't handle something older and deeper and more layered than his fancy furniture. Which also means I can no longer have random sex with women I don't love, because look at my father. Look at him with his miserable teenage-minded girlfriend trying sadly to be sexy. What if I have a chance at the kind of love that's pure unfiltered fuel, a real chance with a gorgeous fire-cracker earth-woman, and what if I just let that chance drift past me and never dare reach for its flame?

Here's another truth: I love my brother. We spent many hours delivering newspapers in the late and moribund light of winter afternoons, and he carried the larger canvas sack. Two gothic-looking houses stood at the end of our route a quarter-mile past any of the others and we had to climb two steep hills to reach them. Many days I was tired and cold and tempted to throw the last couple papers down the sewer, but my brother would tell me to take it easy for a few minutes, and he'd walk alone to those last two houses and I'd sit on the curb by the sewer-grate and wait for him and I loved that interval of rest, the frigid air on my cheeks, the cars rushing past, the thin, bare branches of trees waving like tentacles. I'd see him marching back to me with his upright and purposeful gait and I'd love him and stand up and march home with him and I'll walk with him on the beach every night if he wants me to, and I'll listen to him splash the waves with his tirades and I'll even nod in sympathy on occasion, but, truthfully, he must be suffering. If he really loved Naomi, why would he spend so much time in the musty murk of his basement typing blog-entries destined to be read by no one?

Why don't they have any children?

Why does he do nothing to save their house from dying?

Why, after dinner each night, does he walk in one direction and she run in the other, the distance between them increasing with each step?

The voice on my father's answering machine is a whip. Outside, a siren sounds from a fire-truck blocks away and it's probably not symbolic but it reminds me of my responsibility to get moving. After dropping the rapidly dressing woman back at the dance club, I return to my ridiculous apartment in condo-town, pack a bag and toss it in my car – it's a hybrid, thank you, Old Goat, don't fucking go crazy because I actually utilize the ingenuity of the automobile industry to go places – and then I head east around the bottom of the lake for a slow and agonizing two hours, and then turn north toward Naomi.

When I knock on their door, gently, so as to avoid causing the house to topple over the bluff, my brother and his wife are surprised to see me. "I had a dream," I say, "a vision of your house tumbling down the hillside, rolling end-over-end like a wooden avalanche with dilapidated roof shingles, and finally it crashed against the beach and broke into a billion pieces and a lot of those pieces killed reptiles and birds and spread particulate of lead paint through the sand and the debris engendered a murderous effect for decades. Let me live here with you guys. Let me stay here and fix things. Give me six months. I'll shore up the foundation, re-joist the walls and floors, plant some beach-grass – native species, of course – to slow the erosion of the cliff. Give me six months. I'll give your house another fifty years."

Old Goat looks like he wants to kill me for wasting gasoline driving to his dying house and for imagining the possibility that it doesn't actually have to fall down, that it's thinkable to stave off the twin specter of ecological and domestic disaster, and Naomi, beautiful short Naomi, arches a beautiful, lush eyebrow, but, at last, they nod, more or less in unison, and I'm in.

Now Naomi holds a damp blouse to the breeze so it fills like an airport windsock and she is standing on the side of the porch that's still not too dangerous to stand on – the boards are only partially rotted – and she is not drying the shirt in the dryer in the basement because that is an appliance that no longer functions and, even if it did work, it would use electricity, and she didn't pin it to the clothesline because there's no room left and the blouse is of a turquoise and shimmering substance and I imagine her thinking how in the morning she will mount her five-speed bicycle and soldier off to the kindergarten with renewed determination to save a generation of five-year-olds from the wiles of Spongebob and touch-phones and it seems to me it's not the wind but her spirit filling the contours of the blouse, puffing it, rippling it in the sun.

Naomi toasts marshmallows around a fire-pit in the yard by the front door and Old Goat doesn't eat marshmallows because marshmallows can only be purchased in plastic bags but Naomi likes them and every once in a while she'll find a stick of appropriate length, pierce a marshmallow through its gut as if she's stabbing a vampire's heart, and then she'll wave it over the hot coals and hold it there long enough for the sides to crisp.

"If they catch fire, they remind me of the Olympic Torch," she tells me. "I don't exactly get off on that, but there's a thrill there, I won't deny it. "

Naomi helps me carry two-by-fours while Old Goat is rummaging for balloons on the beach. Naomi dismembers bananas in a blender and hands me a Phillips-head screwdriver and an adjustable wrench. At the market, she catches lemons when I lob them to her. When she naps on the side of the porch she can still nap on, her breasts rise and fall like buoys on the lake. She dances in the kitchen, her legs waving like sea-grass, and when the radio plays Belinda Carlisle, she tosses the thick mane of her hair and says, "When I was little, I wanted to be a Go-Go. Sometimes I still harbor that ambition."

"What's a Go-Go?" asks Old Goat.

One Sunday afternoon, after I tire of watching Old Goat flail at his keyboard, I tiptoe up the ancient, claustrophobic stairs and find Naomi taping drawings made by her students to her refrigerator. She bites her lip as she presses the tape to the corners until the pictures stick. Later, she escorts me to the ice cream parlor near a park that has an abandoned railroad track running through it. She orders what I order, two scoops of Michigan Cherry. Old Goat remains at home blogging. He doesn't eat ice cream because of something about cows and methane and greenhouse gases.

In the morning, showered and fresh for work in a flowered-print dress that drapes nearly to her ankles, a crumb of toast on her lips, Naomi kisses her husband's beard and waves and winks at me. "By the time you get home this afternoon," I tell her, "it will be safe to stand on both sides of the porch."

Over the course of seven months, I have sunk all my money into this house, every dollar I got from the sale of my characterless condo. The edifice is now durable. It will stand for another half-century. There is really nothing more for me to do, but when I leave I will have nowhere to live and no job. I don't often think about the bleakness of those prospects. Neither Old Goat nor Naomi brings up my future. She is grateful I saved her domicile. The Mylar Man is consumed with balloons.

Now, with no more work to do, I walk the beach every night with him and help gather garbage. We don't bring any bags down because there are no plastic bags in the house except on the rare occasions Naomi buys marshmallows and we are sure to find a number of bags while we're down there anyway, or at least we'll find a mylar balloon we can rip a hole in and turn into a bag. We walk in one direction. Naomi runs in the other. I turn around periodically and see if I can spot her in the distance.

"Look at this one," the Mylar Man says.

It's a Happy Birthday balloon, a balloon with the faded images of other balloons on it, like a meta-balloon. The Mylar Man says again what I have heard him say many times: "Happy Death Day is more like it."

I have heard all the Mylar Man's stories and statistics on numerous occasions, how an elementary school class gathered over 500 balloons in just one half-hour of combing through the sand on the Jersey shore; how in late 2006 a *Celebration 2000* balloon was found still intact on a beach in Cape Cod; how approximately 51,000 balloons are collected annually from he shores of Lake Michigan. "Listen," he tells me. "If you studied the chemical composition of this beach, you would find traces of plastic in every single grain of sand. *Every single one.*"

Whether what my brother says is true or not, I have options. I don't have to keep picking up garbage. I don't have to feel guilt. My arms, back and hands have been transformed by all the work on the house. I am steel and strong. There is no one else on this beach except for Naomi who is far away and growing farther with each step. I can plaster one of these balloons across Old Goat's nose and mouth and suffocate him, twist the ribbon around his neck and pull. I can shove him face-down into the lake and hold him underwater until his breath stops bubbling. There are dunes where I can bury him and he won't be found for decades. Unlike mylar, he would decompose. After a suitable period of mourning, Naomi and I could settle down in the newly reconditioned house.

But my brother is already a martyr in his own mind and I won't give him the satisfaction of becoming a public one. Naomi looks often at the new floorboards, the window-screens, the sturdy rails on her porch, and the day is nearing when she will no longer kiss her husband in the mornings when she leaves the house. She will wave and wink at me still, and there will be a day when her leaving will be my leaving too. The Old Goat can remain, in a house that will give him a good many more years as he scours the beach. We will not feel guilty when we are gone. This day is near. Already Naomi walks close to me in the narrow kitchen, brushes her hips against mine, reaches out to touch my sleeve. There is a tide drifting our skins toward each other. I must be patient and float with the rhythms of the lake. It is nearly unbearable but I must not let my desire grow into a storm that overwhelms. I must be a calm body, a tide that waits. When our skins finally meet, we will not separate.

There is a story about mylar balloons I have been waiting to tell my brother. I have known it for a long time. It's a story about how administrators in Grand Central Station grew frustrated about the horde of mylars that had been loosed from the hands of kids in the lobby and journeyed to the ceiling. How the balloons lingered for months, congregated into a veritable convention, obscuring the magnificent starscape that had been painted when the building was first erected. The administrators didn't know how to get the balloons down and contacted some spiritual doppelgangers of my brother, a couple guys who nearly wrecked their marriages when they became obsessed with rescuing plastic bags – "bag-snatching" they called it – from tree-branches. Guys who spent entire weekends combing Greenwich Village with twelve-foot-long aluminum dowels with coat-hooks duct-taped to the ends so they could collect thousands of bags that had once held cosmetics or take-out. "Want to know what these guys came up with?" I ask. "Want to know how they finally got the balloons down?"

The Mylar Man is interested. He tugs shreds of red latex from the sand, a balloon remnant that's been torn to sharp oblong triangles, like dragon fangs. He looks at me. "How'd they do it?" he says.

I wait. The sun is setting over the lake in a swirl of blues, salmons and oranges. I understand what my brother's trying to save. He is beautiful and altruistic and a treasure, but nevertheless a lunatic. Ahead of us is the lighthouse, striped like a barber's pole. Because there have been a lot of balloons today, a lot of digging and clawing, we won't reach it tonight. Soon, we'll reverse course and head back home. Naomi will also turn around and we will journey toward each other. She will become larger and larger as we approach, but she'll still be small, never taller than five feet.

"They clumped a group of other balloons together, a half-dozen or so. Tied the clump to a long string like a giant kite. Then they slathered each balloon with industrial adhesives, buttered their surfaces sticky and sent them to the ceiling. Used the gummy clump like a monstrous fishing rod and, one by one, caught the renegade balloons and pulled them down."

"That's genius," my brother says. "Like a family setting out to recapture its prodigal sons and return them to the fold. I gotta meet these guys."

My brother never wants to meet anyone.

"I'm glad you're here," he tells me as he squints toward the vanishing sun. "I've enjoyed these walks with you."

I'm tempted to pick up a rock and stone him with it. He is a gorgeous Poseidon, shirtless and rippled with the sunset behind him and I don't want to listen to his rants anymore and I don't want him to appreciate me. I am a lousy brother. The temptation to pick up a rock is palpable, quivering. The sound against his temple would be a gift, an inheritance. I want it. I reach downward into the sand. Dig with my fingers and encounter some latex. Blue with a yellow ribbon. I claw it from the beach. Give it to the Mylar Man. He bags it.

Tonight Naomi will not run. Last night, she twisted her ankle. A misstep in the sand, a skitter off an upturned rock. She limped back and iced it for twenty minutes with the cubes leaking through a cloth napkin. She will ice the ankle again tonight instead of running. She is a wounded woman and I have volunteered to keep her company. Old Goat is on the beach. We are watching him from the rebuilt porch as he works his way toward the lighthouse. He is a human combine reaping a harvest of latex and mylar. I imagine he is looking up periodically, missing me, how there is no one tonight for him to show-and-tell.

Naomi sits on a wicker chair, her ankle propped on a throw pillow on a matching chair two feet away. She leans over with a napkin full of ice cubes and applies it to the swelling. The ice melts and leaks in streams down her leg and she fidgets and twists and grimaces and tries to refold napkin corners to contain the leaking. The Mylar Man is far down the beach now, barely visible, a slowly moving dot, smaller, smaller, gone.

"I can't bear to watch him," Naomi says. "That's why I run in the opposite direction."

"Pretty pathetic, isn't he?" I say, and I wonder if I've offended her. She forgets about fussing with the napkin, lets the water stream across her shin. She spends a long minute gazing at the beach, as if she can still see her husband, even though she can't.

"You're making a joke," she says. "You're saying his obsession is ridiculous, that he lacks dignity. But he *is* pathetic. It's sad. He can't clean the whole planet. He can't even clean this stretch of beach."

Naomi's back curves as she presses the leaking ice to her ankle, and all the fire has gone out of her shoulders. She is uncomfortable, twisting more and fidgeting. What she's telling me is that my brother is also too big of a beach to clean. Too deep a wound. She can't dive into it anymore, the canyon of his hurt, and she can't save him and she's ready to give up. She wants someone who will take on tasks that aren't hopeless. A man who can save a home.

I point my finger upward and draw a heart in the air.

She shakes her head, looks out at the beach, then turns back toward me.

A ribbon of hair falls across her face and scratches her cheek. She can't do anything about it because her hands are holding the ice, and I reach toward her. I lift the strand and when she looks at me her eyes are full. The sun is a ripe blaze. We know how long her husband will be gone, two hours at least.

Naomi is all heat now, still gazing at me, the ice running a river over her shin. If our skins touch, we will not separate. "My back aches," she says.

I know what she wants.

DROWNING SUPERMAN

Calista's immature in some ways. I'm immature in other ways. It's not a contest, but it's hell when I lose.

Often, I lose.

Our vacation has been one putrid smoking disaster after another. Every time something new goes wrong, I calm myself with the reminder it was Calista's idea to spend seventy-five hundred dollars to rent a cottage infested with ticks, mice and spiders for a week on Martha's Vineyard. Her idea to endure seven straight days of over-priced restaurants, every one of which is too crowded and takes forever.

Waiting too long for a forty-two dollar lobster and its microwaved potato companion is not the same thing as waiting for sex. The build-up, the anticipation of peeling somebody's thong off, of watching a pair of nipples tune in like a radio signal – when these things come to fruition, the irritation of the previous delay can evaporate. Not so with food that when it arrives tastes only slightly more appetizing than truck tires.

What exacerbates the disaster of our vacation is Jesse, our four-year-old, who's been crying like a faucet most of the week. He's not a bad kid. He is, in fact, a tremendous kid – commits all manner of adorable pre-school behaviors like calling Frankenstein *Freakenstein* when our neighbor dressed up as the spark-plugged blockhead last Halloween – but he's also on the fast track to psychological weed addiction and years of regularly scheduled therapy because he gets far too much attention from his parents. Calista and I focus on him in order to avoid focusing on each other. We know Jesse is our best thing, both our lone successful group-project and our sole remaining chance for redemption, so we try to outdo each other during our special one-on-one times with him. If Calista takes him to the pseudo-farm where kids can pet unhealthy looking goats and llamas, I have to escort him to the balls-out zoo where the orangutans enjoy frolicking with their genitals. If I escort him to the zoo, she takes him to an amusement park and sits next to him on the kiddie rides and wins him a four-foot high stuffed aardvark.

That's how we wound up on Martha's Vineyard. Calista called a truce.

We have to put an end to this arms race, she said. We need to do something as a *family*.

So we eat expensive lazily-prepared food as a family, except Jesse doesn't eat his. He's so damn hungry waiting, and whining, and waiting, and whining, that he invariably fills up on bread or his fingernails or some old cheese and crackers from the beach bag Calista demands I lug everywhere, and by the time his seventeen-dollar plate of buttered spaghetti arrives at the table, he has nothing to offer it but sneering disdain, which is fair. I bear no ill will toward my son for whining about how starving he is for several hours and then picking at only a couple pieces of his pasta. I am angry only at Calista who glares at me with her nefarious teacher-eyes, the ones that make her fifth-graders feel like if they leave their seats to get a tissue, razor-sharp scimitars will descend from the ceiling and shred them to confetti.

We should've just told the waitress to bring the food to him in a box, she says. We're going to have to box it up now anyway and bring it home.

I'm not one of your students, I say. Don't lecture me.

Traveling to Martha's Vineyard involves a forty-five minute ride to Detroit Metro, then a two-hour flight from Detroit to Boston, then another two hours with all our bulky luggage on a foul-smelling bus from Logan to Woods Hole, capped off with another forty-five minute ride, this time on a ferry to Vineyard Haven so congested it's a struggle to find enough seats together and we have to schlep our luggage up and down several sets of stairs, so let's not talk about how we could've just rented a cottage on Lake Michigan for a quarter of the price and driven three quick hours up north and fallen asleep immediately in a hammock. Instead, let's just say the root of the boxing-the-food controversy is that Calista felt it necessary to formulate a strategy so Jesse would be bearable during his maiden voyage on an airplane.

This is the difference between Calista and me. She always wants to plan for disasters because she believes in the high probability of disasters and that you can lessen their impact if you prepare for them. I believe that's nonsense. I believe you can generally avoid disasters through blind random luck and, if they happen to strike you, you won't know when or where or to what extent, so preparing is just a waste of energy. Plus, preparing usually encompasses some incarnation of a large bag, like the beach-bag, and though Calista stuffs it with all the lingering anxieties from her worrisome childhood, I'm the one who inevitably winds up carrying it wherever we go. There's too much, I think whenever I'm lugging the bag like a sweaty, shoulder-aching Santa Claus, too much in the world that's unknowable. You can't control every damn variable.

Still, as part of the airplane strategy, Calista spent two weeks glorifying all the wonders of modern air travel, toting Jesse outside on her hip before putting him to bed and pointing at the sky. You see the stars up there, she cooed to him, you see those stars that look like they're moving? Those are airplanes cruising through the night. They are warm on the inside, and safe. That's where we're going to be. Floating through the sky. And you'll have your own seat, next to a window, and the shade for the window will be made of hard plastic and you'll be able to pull it up and down all by yourself, and Jesse, listen, here's the best part. When you sit in your own seat, you'll also have your very own table. It will be attached to the seat in front of you and there will be a little latch that will be easy for you to open and then you'll be able to unfold your table all by yourself. And, when they serve you food, guess what, Jesse, guess what? The snack will come in a box. That's right, they'll serve you a snack that comes in a box!

Personally, I failed to see the thrill involved with boxed food, but Jesse was enamored so, okay, play that up, Calista, if you think it'll make the kid happy. Except, when three days before we were scheduled to depart on our glorious airplane with its very own plastic shades and tray-tables, Calista served us a tofu and green beans stir-fry in boxes she'd bought from a restaurant supply store, I thought things were going too far. Did we run out of plates, I said, or are we boxing the tofu up to take to a restaurant and eat it there?

Not funny, Jay, she said. Can't you see Jesse loves this? Can't you lighten up and have some fun?

Jesse, I said to my son, some day you will kiss a girl in the backseat of a car. She will be chewing gum and you'll be able to tell by how she sucks in a pull of breath right before your lips meet that she wants you to kiss her as much as you want her to kiss you, and that will be something to love. That will be something that's fun.

That's not something appropriate to tell a four-year-old, Calista said.

For three days, my wife served my son all his meals in boxes and damn if he didn't love it, and damn if the kid wasn't so excited on the airplane he hardly noticed his ears popping during takeoff, and damn if he didn't whine once and practically had his first orgasm when the flight attendant at last placed the cardboard-shrouded ham-and-cheese-on-a-damp-croissant on the tray-table that Jesse had folded down all by himself, and damn if at least a half-dozen people didn't compliment us on how well-behaved our beautiful child was and, boy, we must be wonderful parents, goodness, how *do* we do it?

To this point, such triumphs constitute Calista's happiest

moments of the vacation. Here is Calista at baggage claim glowing like a fake tan as yet another prosperous-looking older woman saunters over to tell us how terrific our boy is – what a little gentleman! – and here, by way of contrast, is Calista dark and menacing when I insist that, no, we will not ask the waitress to serve Jesse's meal to him in a box.

Why not, she says. He'll eat it. I guarantee if it comes in a box, he'll eat it.

Because I don't care if he never eats again, I refuse to allow us to be that family that represents everything that's wrong with the world.

What's wrong with making the dining experience a little bit fun, a little bit special for our son? How is that everything wrong with the world?

That's the problem, Calista, you don't know.

Oh, fuck you, my wife says to me in front of my son in a crowded restaurant. Fuck you, Jay, she says. You're not human.

What Calista doesn't understand is that when I say you can't control every variable, I mean it like it's a measure of truth that will hinder every step I take the rest of my life. I bear the mark of that truth in a scar shaped like a compressed lightning bolt, white and fat, beneath my right knee.

Halfway through my sophomore year in college, I have a shot to be the starting varsity leftfielder, but the coaches have concerns about my defense. Has trouble tracking fly balls, one of them says. Arm's only adequate, proclaims another. These, in my opinion, are falsehoods of the highest order. When they finally put me in, I'm determined to prove them wrong. Hit me a fly ball, I chant under my breath every time an opposing batter comes to the plate. Force me to make a throw. Try to run on me, I dare you.

In the last inning of a scoreless game, a left-handed batter lofts a medium range pop-up, a little slicer toward the foul line. It's potentially a run-scoring double that means we will lose. But I read it from the crack of the bat, before the crack actually, read it from the pitcher's release of the outside pitch and the lean of the batter's weight. I'm on my horse and get to the ball in time to line up behind it and catch it running forward, face-level just like I'm supposed to, so I can generate momentum for a throw to the plate. The runner on third tags up and sprints home and, with one gracefully executed crow-hop, my throw is artwork. It even *sounds* right, a sniper's bullet, low and fast, and it will shoot into the catcher's mitt and eliminate the base-runner as efficiently as a mob-hit.

Except here comes Cal Pulliam, dim-witted underperforming third baseman, barrel-chested, Nebraskan and soap opera handsome, who will soon be suspended for three semesters for plagiarizing an economics paper. He's slumped all year at the plate, slept with more women on campus than anybody else on the team, and muffed nearly as many ground balls. Our coaches pretend to adore him because they don't want to admit the mistake they made signing him to a full scholarship. It doesn't matter how badly he plays, he'll be in the line-up every day.

When I unfurl my symphonic masterpiece of a throw, there's no logical reason in the known universe to cut it off. The throw is on line and perfect and the runner streaking home will be out by five feet. The catcher, whose job it is to shout *Cut Four!* if he believes the throw should be intercepted, is as silent as Cal will be next month when the ethical board presents him with the evidence of his cheating and sentences him back to Nebraska for a year-and-a-half. Not a syllable escapes his mouth, yet here comes Cal Pulliam's glove, rising unaccountably upward. Prior to Calista's scimitar eyes, it is the most vile thing I will ever see. Cal doesn't even properly cut the ball off, just nips it and redirects it wildly into foul territory. The winning run scores in a glide. We lose and are somber. None of the coaches say a thing to Cal about his bonehead play and my resplendent throw is forgotten, irrelevant. I still must prove my worth to the coaches and, the next day I dive after a meaningless line-drive during batting practice. My spike catches in a sprinkler drain. A harsh and prolonged tearing emanates from my leg and I leave pieces of ligament and cartilage all over the field.

Jesse's favorite toy is a Superman figurine. It isn't made of plastic, but it's not metal either. Maybe it's metal covered with some kind of rubberized paint. The thing that's important is that it doesn't float. We use it to teach Jesse how to swim. Back at the kiddie pool in the municipal park in Michigan, Calista or I would sit on the edge and toss the figurine into the deepest part of the water, about two-and-a-half feet. Jesse scampered after it and had to learn how to hold his breath and dip his head underwater in order to fish around with his fingers and retrieve it. Throwing Superman into shallow water and watching our son rescue him is one of the few activities Calista and I enjoy sharing. After we do it for an hour or so, if we can get Jesse to go home and take a nap, Calista and I might even make love. We brought the Superman with us to Martha's Vineyard with the hope of tossing it into salt water so Jesse could search for it and exhaust himself. It was our intention then, while he napped, to make love.

Here's the problem. The house we rented is in an old whaling-village-now-shopping-mecca called Edgartown. There's a gorgeous public beach nearby that we can easily catch a shuttle to called Katama, also known as South Beach. It's not exactly the kind of isolated dune-and-clay-cliff paradise you think of when you think of Martha's Vineyard though. Not the kind of place where you can stroll with your wife and kid for an hour and run into only one recovering-alcoholic-slash-playwright perched on a lonesome rock, thinking of the denouement for his next script and how he can weave in the evaporation of his second marriage. South Beach isn't a postcard like that. It's towel-to-towel crowded and smells like somebody dumped a million gallons of sunscreen onto the seaweed. Popular enough to merit trendy sweatshirts trumpeting itself as a happening party spot for Ivy League kids on the island for the summer to staff gourmet ice cream shops. It's a scene. A bright and shining landscape of kids with no homework playing hackeysack to a continuous James Taylor soundtrack.

That's all fine though. Even if the crowded nature of South Beach means I have to lug the plus-size bag stuffed with a dozen vials of combo UV-35-and-bug-repellent gel, numerous clothing changes for Jesse, enough towels for several extended families, and a year's supply of cheese and crackers an extra half-mile in order to find a ten-by-ten-foot patch of sand for us to colonize, still, it's the ocean, and we don't have that in Michigan. I also have no problem looking at girls in bikinis playing hackeysack. Girls who like to prove their mettle to their stoned and pseudo-hippie boyfriends by sprinting toward the water and plunging into the raucous waves. That's another thing I enjoy watching, all that sprinting and plunging, but the raucous waves also present a difficulty – Jesse's terrified of them. He won't dare attempt to wade into them with me, or even to let me hold him safely above the water as I walk into them, tottering on my balky knee.

Calista's not much for waves either. She'd rather sit on a blanket and choose from one of the fourteen novels she's packed into the bag while Jesse eats one of the boxed snacks she prepared for him, which means that even though Calista's more beautiful than any of the college girls, she doesn't sprint and plunge so I can't watch and admire. The beach is basically a bust. Jesse can only handle Katama for about an hour, which means my shoulders and back barely recover from lugging the bag from shuttle to sand before it's time to start the return-schlep from sand to shuttle. And without Jesse rescuing Superman from the water, there's no chance for sex with Calista. There's only her snarl.

This is another philosophical difference between Calista and me. She's against having sex when we're fighting. She won't be intimate with me when she's disgusted with me. I need to feel closer, she'll say. Get to know me first. Make an effort.

I, on the other hand, believe sex brings us closer, that when we're physically vulnerable with each other, we can become emotionally vulnerable too. Human beings need touch, I plead. That's why interns get paid to hold sick babies in hospital nurseries. If humans don't get touched, we wither and die.

Let's not wither, I say. Let's not die.

But Calista's not having it.

One morning we hear on the radio that the surf at Katama will be relatively mild. Calista takes three hours to pack the bag and we again make the pilgrimage. The surf is not mild. It is as before, raucous and frolicking. Jesse will go nowhere near it. I spend an hour building sandcastles with him while Calista reads. I'm not good at building sandcastles. Back and hamstrings sore from lugging the bag, I don't want to bend down or squat in the sand. I help Jesse build what amounts to a series of shapeless mounds of mud by observing, by standing with my arms crossed and boring myself to numbness. Get down in the sand with him, get your hands dirty, Calista yells at me, but I pretend not to hear her as I scout around for cute college girls diving into the waves. When I notice a particularly athletic quartet, I tell Jesse sandcastle time is over and drop him back at the towels with Calista. I need to go for a swim, I say, work the kinks out.

I have a fantasy that I will cavort in and out of the surf like a dolphin and pop up in the midst of the college girls like a pizza guy in a porn video. I don't have any intentions of initiating physical contact with them, but I want them to admire me, to note that even though I am fifteen years older than they are, my chest still ripples in the sun, my shoulders still represent something bronze and powerful. I do my dolphin thing and hope the tide will buffet the girls toward me but it doesn't and they don't come within twenty yards. I grow cold and parched and sunburned and emerge from the waves like our planet's first ever amphibian stretching out his flippers, tired of water, dreaming of feet.

When I look up, I see a tall slender dickhead talking to my wife. He has the exact look of a man who owns a four-million-dollar house but dresses in raggedy t-shirts and shorts to prove he still relates to the masses. Jesse's eating cheese and crackers and Calista's smiling at the dickhead in a way she hasn't smiled at me for months, in a way that demonstrates more majesty than the roiling surf, more sustenance than the sun. I forget about hoping to evolve. I will beat this tall man's ass all the way back to his Land Rover.

Fortunately, the man drifts on to paddle his designer kayak to Nantucket or perform some other glossy exploit and I say to Calista, Who's that dude and what was he doing by our towels? What's he coveting in our bag?

Just a guy who lives nearby, Calista says, clearly annoyed I'm acting like an adolescent. He was telling me about another beach, she says, a nature preserve called Long Point. He says it's the best place on the island to take kids, the best place for swimming.

Oh, I say, that sounds good. But I'm thinking I will kill that dude. I will steal a bottle of expensive Zinfandel from his climate-controlled wine cellar and crack him in the head with it, then overturn his kayak and drown him.

There's no shuttle to Long Point. We rent bicycles because the dickhead told Calista that's the best option. We hitch one of those moon-tent trailers onto the back of my bike for Jesse to ride in and he loves it, plus the in-case-of-every-possible-emergency-known-to-humankind bag fits neatly in beside him so I don't have to carry it on my back. The ride to the preserve's entrance is only about eight miles from Edgartown and it's relatively flat and there's a smoothly paved bike-path. I'm beginning not to hate the dickhead. The Superman is tucked somewhere in the vast reaches of the bag and I am happily anticipating tossing it into what's been described as an idyllic freshwater pond, no waves, warm temperature, pebbleless sand. Calista and I will watch Jesse fetch it and I imagine that later we will pedal back to the mice-infested rental and he will nap and we will initiate our own kind of sprinting and plunging intimacy and our vacation will be saved.

Except the road from the preserve entrance to the pond is four additional miles of soft dry dirt. After one half of one mile, my knee is fried. The bike spins and fish-tails and clouds of dust choke Jesse in his tent-trailer and he coughs and cries. Calista zooms ahead, yelling back that she'll pick out a good spot on the beach. It's ninety degrees and dead-ass humid. The wheels of my bike skid and sink in the sand. My knee is on its way to swelling to the size of a watermelon. I will wake up tomorrow morning in a kind of pain that will feel like someone whacked me with a crowbar. I estimate the number of ensuing days I will not be able to walk at three. I want to cough and cry like Jesse, but I don't. It's okay, I tell him. You're getting out of there. Out of that cage.

I stop the bike without braking because we are hardly moving, unstrap Jesse from his dusty prison, and hoist him onto my shoulders. He likes to ride up there and stops crying. He weighs forty-five pounds and my orthopedist has warned me against gaining weight because each additional pound I carry is equivalent to six pounds of pressure on the knee with the missing cartilage, six pounds of pressure on bone grinding against bone. I tell my son he's going to have to hold on around my neck, thereby semi-strangling me, because I will need both hands on the handlebars while I push the bike. We begin to walk the remaining three-and-a-half miles.

It's awful, but I can actually lean some of the weight against the bike and it functions in similar fashion to one of those wheeled walkers old people use. The hardest part is keeping Jesse balanced, and sometimes, I have to hold one of his feet so he doesn't fall off my shoulders as I simultaneously try to push bike and trailer with one hand. If I want to keep everything in sync, I can't stop to swipe at the streams of sweat oozing into my eyes so I try to embody the sting and keep pressing forward, one foot after another trudging through the dirt. I ignore the howls from my knee and work to establish a kind of cadence. I will not lose to Calista this time. I will keep moving. I think about the dickhead who put me in this situation. I think about Cal Pulliam the plagiarizing moron. I plod forward. I will keep moving. I will not lose to Calista. Not now.

Eventually, wondering where the hell we are, she pedals back to find us. When she spots the pathetic slow-moving sight of us, she hops off her bike. I'm sorry, she says. Here, let me push the bike with the trailer. You push this one.

I do. The rest of the odyssey takes close to an hour. We don't talk but I feel indebted. Jesse nearly falls asleep on my shoulders, and I have to keep shaking him awake so he can hang on around my neck. But I want to sleep, Daddy, he pleads. Please, Daddy, I want to sleep.

At last, we round a bend and, about a quarter-mile away, what looks like an enormous garden of neon and pastel beach umbrellas sprouts into view. We park the bikes at a bike-rack and because removing Jesse from my shoulders at this point would be akin to peeling duct tape off the hairs on my thighs, he stays up there and Calista lugs the beach bag. The last quarter-mile nearly murders me, but we make it. The pond is as advertised. Exquisite and calm and surrounded by lush vegetation and soaring seafowl. We rush into it immediately. The water is fresh and soothing and, as Calista watches Jesse, I swim for a few minutes far from the madding crowd and I gaze up at a sky that seems happy to embrace every fucked up thing about me and I float and float.

We stay at the beach for hours. For much of the time, I lie half-reclined in the water, my legs submerged, which seems to mitigate some of the knee-swelling. Jesse splashes next to me and builds shapeless sandcastles. Calista massages my shoulders. Somehow we are a family again. We are having so much fun we don't even pull out the Superman until late afternoon. We will be leaving soon and Calista says, Do you mind playing with Jesse for, like, fifteen minutes? I just want to finish this book. Ten more pages.

No problem, I say, and I mean it. And when, after a couple dozen throws, I heave the figurine too long and it plunks too deep in the pond and Jesse comes bawling out of the water saying he couldn't get it and Superman's gone, he's gone forever, and Calista's eyes panic and initiate a rapid boil because this is the one emergency she's not prepared for – we don't have a Superman duplicate or even a Batman and the toy was a gift in the first place and we don't know where to get another one – I say again, No problem, I'll find it.

It's important to know I am in love with my son's bushy eyebrows, the curves of muscle in his back and legs. I also adore the pair of birthmarks beneath Calista's bottom-left Achilles tendon. The two of them, my son and wife, are the most wondrous sights on the beach, more picturesque than the pond, the birds. When I threw the Superman too far, I was not trying to relive my masterpiece throw or attempting to demonstrate the continued existence of my arm strength. I swear it. Nor was I distracted because Long Point, populated not with college girls but with young mothers like Calista, is a far more sexually dangerous place for me, and that hovering not twenty feet to my right was a particularly attractive mom in a bright orange two-piece with a stomach flat and sun-baked, and that just when I was cocking my arm to throw she happened to be bending over and packing her own family's overstuffed bag. No, when I overthrew the Superman, I was, in fact, pleasantly bored watching seagulls loop-de-loop, and the thing just slipped.

I plot my search as if it's a child who's disappeared, drafting in my mind a thirty-by-thirty foot grid in which somewhere Superman lies below the surface. Methodically, I pick my way across the grid, raking every square inch of sand with my fingers. I am confident, but careful too. Even as Jesse, inconsolable, curls up in Calista's arms on a towel, I try to avoid the creation of upsurging plumes of sand, clouds that will obscure my vision of everything below. The process is worrisome because I don't have all night. There is still the perilous hike back to the main road, the eight-mile bike ride after that. There is still the fact that tomorrow morning my knee will feel nine months pregnant and I will not be able to walk for three days, yet I relish this challenge.

Calista is stroking Jesse's hair and they are counting on me to accomplish the rescue. I will not fail. Superman, invulnerable Kryptonian that he is, may nonetheless remain underwater too long for his lungs to continue breathing. He may not survive this debacle, he may drown, but I will not leave him here for some other kid not nearly as magical as Jesse to find. I will not abandon Superman to be preserved in ice when the pond freezes over in the winter, his rubberized eyes wide and staring.

I am not leaving until I recover this body.

The woman in the orange bathing suit heads back to the parking lot, but my eyes do not follow her. I can hear my son sniffling on the beach as I peer into the saltless water. I walk gingerly. I won't make clouds. I focus my vision and tune out the gulls, feel for the current to tell my fingers where to search next.

Somewhere, the hero is here.

BASEMENTS

Mike D's: We invent ourselves here, and try again when we fuck up. We are the offspring of our parents' migrations to the suburbs and we orbit around New York City, claiming it and afraid of it. In our homes, we are moles, living for the rooms underground. We inhabit them and stake them as ours, pieces of our parents' dreams we want to own for ourselves – the mildewed foundations of our houses. The primary piece of furniture in Mike's basement – a bumper-pool table – becomes our altar. We circle it and play the angles. The Yankees strum a symphony on a TV with a busted color tube. Everything in the game looks green. Sparky Lyle's face looks green. Phil Rizzuto's sportsjacket. This is where the first and only hickey takes place, on a school night, on a vinyl couch with a mohair blanket. The cushions squeak. Mike D wrestles with his girl Lizette on another couch five feet away. The TV is not on and we are listening to music low on the stereo, a Jackson Browne album. The record pleads for someone to *stay-ay-ay* just a little bit longer in a voice squeakier than my little sister's. Claudia, who has narrow breasts and sports a faint mustache above her upper lip, whispers, I'm going to mark you.

Her teeth poke my neck like the tines of a fork, digging bloodworms from my skin. Moonlight sifts through the window we propped open so the girls could sneak in, and Claudia unbuttons my pants and says, You've never done this before, have you? I lie but she doesn't buy it. Her fingers are gentle. Lizette giggles from the other couch and I wish it were a different night, a weekend, wish there were more of us. I wish I could hear the clack and plunk of sticks and balls. I wish I could hear Johnny trash-talking and Lennie saying he's full of shit and the underlying bass-line of green baseball games.

Everyone is too young to drive but Mike D. steals his father's car because Lizette and Claudia need to get home and nobody has money for a taxi. For our initial getaway, Mike puts the car in neutral and Lizette and I push it out of his driveway so it won't make any noise. While this happens, Claudia urinates beneath a hedge of blooming forsythia. I'm still feeling the tattoo of her fingers and her teeth and other than during a sixth grade camping trip – when any girl who had to piss hid deep within a grove of trees with at least one other girl keeping guard – I've never known a female to relieve herself outside. None of us are drunk and when we hit the road we drive fourteen miles-an-hour and don't get caught.

The graffiti Claudia leaves on my neck takes the shape of two purple welts. Mike D. calls them rope burns. She lives at the bottom of a neighborhood called Battle Hill. I am not afraid to go to Battle Hill, but we don't talk on the way to her house because everybody's worried Mike will plow into another car and injure us for life. I am relieved when we drop her off at the curb. While Lizette whispers something to Mike in the front seat and touches him somewhere, Claudia stands next to the car and says to me, I'm glad I'm the one who did it. I'm glad I'm the one who cleaned your pipes.

I wonder what this means and Mike D. releases the brake and nudges the car forward while Claudia's still standing there waiting for me to respond. The rear tire rolls over her foot and she screams and screams and screams.

Johnny A.M. to the P.M's: For boys, it is a post and pre-dancing era. We are Italian mostly, and Irish, with a Jew here and there. We will never admit it, but for years John Travolta was our hero. He wore a T-Birds jacket with the collar high and sharp and he nailed Olivia Newton-John after she instructed him to, *Tell me about it, Stud.* He pulled a bunch of other lesser-known chicks too, in that other movie while he was wearing a ridiculous white suit. We could never figure that out, but it doesn't matter because disco has wheezed its final breath and older kids who at one point memorized The Hustle don't want to admit things like that ever happened. Hip hop is an exotic woman with crazy hips we want to flirt with. Her mouth is sexy and bold. It is not enough for us to put on a record and sit on a couch. Not enough for us to pretend we are potheads and say, Dude, this is so cool.

We make a pilgrimage to Fordham Road and buy two turntables and a mixing board, carpeted speakers with bass woofers the size of globes. We look like idiots when we try and stuff them into Johnny's mother's station wagon. It's forty minutes of tying other shit to the roof and folding down seats and sweating like tourists and people on the street looking at us, three very white and clueless stooges begging to get our asses kicked. We all crowd into the front for the drive home and Davey has to sit on my lap. I can't help breathing into his neck and we are embarrassed and sweating and broke, and we will never tell anyone this story.

Purchasing electronic equipment in the South Bronx requires balling up our allowances in our socks and shopping at electronics stores that look like pharmacies. Nothing will have price-tags. Everything will be cheaper if we agree to buy items without boxes or paperwork. Johnny will be the one who will urge us to turn our backs and walk out of the store if we don't like the price. If we make the journey at night there will be hookers in abundance who will be a lot prettier than we imagined they would be. Johnny will describe how he tried to get a blowjob from one of them in the backseat when his brother was driving the station wagon but it didn't work out. Why not, someone will ask, blew your wad in your jeans? Fuck you, Johnny will say. No one will believe he ever even made an attempt.

We will pretend to rock parties until the break of dawn. We will pretend lots of the kinds of girls who think we are dull – the kinds who prefer lacrosse players who slant-park their Toyota hatchbacks and have parents who pay for SAT prep classes – will come to our blow-out bashes. They will mostly be blond and will dance with each other until they tire and then they will search for us in dark corners for groping and other activities of their own devising. We will prove we are not dull.

In preparation, G-Lover will show us how to work the needles back and forth across the backbeat to make scratching sounds. We will all look very beautiful with headphones covering one ear only. Johnny will make out with my sort-of girlfriend at a New Year's Eve party. He won't be sorry, but I will forgive him and not her. Johnny's mother will sometimes bring pitchers of lemonade downstairs and will say, Don't do that to your records, that's how you ruin them. Johnny's sister Maria Louisa is very cute and says hi to me shyly in the hallways at school. It's an extraordinary privilege to stand behind her at the water fountain, but that is as far as it will go. When I'm playing shortstop, I backpedal on pop-ups and Johnny comes sprinting in from leftfield and calls me off. I let him and that's how we win games.

The basement is well organized, its orange shelves filled with old children's books and board-games like Trouble and Sorry. High up, two shelves are devoted solely to Johnny's baseball cards. No one ever talks about them but one notebook is labeled Hall-of-Famers and there's a mint Mickey Mantle in there from the early '50s. It's tempting to steal it. To fuck Johnny up on some tequila and slip the card out of its protective sleeve and into my pocket. Johnny said he played strip ping-pong one time with a snobby girl named Harriet from my chemistry class and that is bullshit. She is known for wearing paisley scarves and other pretentious accoutrements and he should pay for lying like that.

There are two hockey sticks in the corner no one ever uses. The window is left open so the music can bump the whole neighborhood. One Saturday night, when other less worthy kids are crawling their hands toward crotches of girls who should have nothing to do with them, it happens just like G showed us. Record and palm connect like lovers and the beat revolves backward, then forward, then backward again. I release it graceful and free, yearning, like a rooftop pigeon – *chikka-chikka-chik* – right on time with the rhythm. Johnny's mouth opens in wonder. The sidewalks outside vibrate. The streetlights bust a groove.

Lennie Ross's: He and Davey are the token Jews, but does that matter? It's all about the bench-press. Lennie's a goddamn animal. He will lift weights every day if no one tells him to cease and desist. Davey too. Freaks. They talk about girls as if they actually get them, as if it's as easy as dunking on the eight-foot rim at the elementary school across the street. His house has a TV with cable and MTV videos are present, but it's background. Except for Aerosmith. Everybody stops for *Walk This Way*.

We all hid down there once, quiet with the videos on, but no sound. It was summer. We were pool-hopping, a frequent activity consisting of jumping a fence and sliding into somebody's pool after midnight, hanging there underwater up to our necks, and whispering until we started shivering. We were wraiths, silvery phantoms in the dark. On Lennie's street, the pools were heated. Sometimes we didn't shiver for hours. Dogs barked far away and people watched late-night talk shows. We ducked and slithered into their pools and they never knew.

G-Lover only came with us that one time. Skittery like a squirrel. I'm Black, he said, I'll get shot. Jews don't own guns, Lennie said. We negotiate. He snuck upstairs and got everybody towels from his mother's linen closet. G's was ugly, with a picture of a dog with its tongue hanging out. Don't laugh, Lennie said, that used to be my favorite towel. I got laid on that towel at Jones Beach. Your mother got laid on that towel at Jones Beach, Johnny said. G-Lover laughed like it was the first joke he'd ever heard. He was running-back fast and played centerfield.

We went to a house we'd been to a million times.

The Gaynors' was awesome because there was a corner of the fence that was wide open to accommodate an ancient apple tree.

It was easy to monkey up the trunk and then drop silently from an over-hanging branch into the water. The pool was warm like a bath. We could chill there all night, listening to apples splash in the deep end. Leslie Gaynor was the hottest Jewish girl anyone had ever seen. We were always hoping she'd emerge from the sliding glass doors on her back porch, peel off a towel, and skinny-dip. Davey would later say he did her, but no one ever confirmed it.

The Gaynors had a skimmer, an automatic vacuum cleaner they left on while they were sleeping. It whirred around the pool like a spaceship, spitting chlorine and clunking into floating apples and pushing them toward the filter. We emptied the filter-baskets under the stars, dumping the apples near the trunk of the tree by the fence as if that's where they'd naturally fallen. Sometimes we fished frogs and turtles and drowned mice out of filters too. If we could do good deeds like that for the owners of the pools we trespassed in, we did them.

The night G-Lover came with us, the water was caressing us like some hot chick's soft lips, everything lush and warm and still, our baseball dirt dissolving in the water and getting sucked up by the whirring vacuum as it scooted around the pool. This is fucking beautiful, G said. Your mother's fucking beautiful, Johnny said. G laughed loud like we were on the back of the bus after trouncing some weak squad of hitless wonders and Davey hissed to shut the fuck up but it was too late.

The sliding glass doors opened and Leslie's fat father yelled, Who's out there? What's going on? I'm calling the police.

We had a plan for that kind of situation, which was to morph into Saturday morning cartoon characters and duck our heads underwater. Hold our collective breath for forty-five seconds and then raise our eyes just above the surface and hope whoever thought he heard something would start thinking it was all in his head. He needed to stop smoking that cheeb or to get more sleep, and then he'd go construct a sophisticated salami sandwich with gourmet deli mustard to calm himself down and everything would be chill again. Except G-Lover didn't know about the plan. As soon as he heard Leslie's fat father yelling, he took off. Bounded out of the pool and scurried up the tree and over the fence. Fuck, Johnny yelled because he knew we were all busted. Everybody scrambled after G and Leslie's pops was spitting and sputtering and erupting like a huge and loud volcano: I see you! I see you kids! Get the hell off my property!

G sprinted like the ghost of Gayle Sayers and we all ran back to Lennie's house and hustled down to the basement and laughed our asses completely off the continent. Then we heard an engine tune down as a car pulled into the driveway. Shit, Lennie said, Kill the light, and he climbed up to the casement to look out the window. He said it was Gaynor, fuming, huffing out of his stupendous marshmallow white Cadillac with the dog towel in his hands. Damn, G, he said, you left your towel?

Man, I wasn't thinking about a towel. I was thinking about not getting shot by that fat dude.

Lennie shook his head in the gloom and I thought he was about to start talking about Jews negotiating again, but he seemed too nervous for that. That's an old towel, he said. I had it back in day-camp. My mom sewed my name in there.

Fuck, Johnny said. Why'd you run anyway, G?

I'm not white like you, man. They could hang me from that apple tree.

If Johnny were about to make another mother joke, he didn't. I thought about G in centerfield, calling Johnny off on balls in the gap, sometimes when he couldn't reach them. How they'd roll to the fence and our coach would rail at him, smack his palm against G's temple and say, Use your head, for crissakes, use your goddamn head out there. You have one, right?

We heard the doorbell ring.

Everyone be quiet, Lennie said. No one move.

It was dark and damp. Cold cement floor. Nothing to shelter us but one beat-up couch and the bench for the bench-press.

Our shorts were still wet and we were shaking. Johnny turned on the TV to create a little more light, but muted the sound. The doorbell rang again and we heard Lennie's father clomp down the stairs from his bedroom and say, Hang on, hold your horses, hang on. He opened the door and then the voices were muffled, but we could tell Gaynor was pissed. We watched Janet Jackson dance provocatively in silence, our ears straining to pick up what was happening outside the front door. She was wearing something vampirish, black, rubbery-looking and low-cut. It was enthralling. I stopped listening to the muffled voices. G-Lover didn't.

After a few minutes, we heard the door slam and Lennie reported that Gaynor, towel-less, was headed back to his car, muttering. He drove off and Mr. Ross opened the door to the basement, began to walk down the stairs. Yo, I'm gonna bust out, G said. I'm going home.

Just chill, bro, Johnny said. We'll be all right.

You'll be all right.

We could feel G vibrating, itching to run again, but he didn't. Everyone stayed quiet. Janet Jackson opened her mouth to moan and it was spectacular. The round hole of it in the dark. Len, turn on the light, his father said.

He was holding the dog-towel. I don't want you guys trespassing anymore, he said. It's dangerous. I lied for you, Lennie. Told Bob Gaynor you were upstairs sleeping. Had been for hours. Said we sold the towel at a garage sale years ago. Got seventy-five cents for it. Know why I did that?

No one answered. Johnny respectfully turned off the TV.

Because Bob Gaynor's a jerk. Said he saw a Black kid in his pool. That's all he said, a Black kid and a gang of hoodlums. Said if he'd had a gun, he would've fired it. Would've been within his rights. That's bullshit, but one of you could have been dead. Probably G, because that's where he would have aimed.

G nodded.

This nonsense stops, Lennie's father said. It stops tonight.

He threw the towel at Lennie. If you want to swim, Mr. Ross said, go to the club. Better yet, go to Jones Beach. That's where the girls are anyway.

He went back upstairs. Lennie and Davey began to lift weights. Prince danced and so did Madonna. Stevie Nicks in her hippie sandals. Give me a spot, G said, throwing more weight on the bar than any of the rest of us could lift. Don't let this shit fall on my chest.

Davey's: As a crew, we only spend time there once. After a hurricane, his yard floods and nine inches of water seep through the floor. Six of us join Davey and work for five hours moving furniture and rolling up sopping wet rugs. They weigh excessive amounts that challenge our hamstrings. We pull and grunt and manage to drag them outside so we can spread them in the sun to dry. Mop an ugly grey river out through the garage. There's no snow anywhere and not even the idea of it, but Johnny asks if he can borrow a pair of cross-country skis Davey hasn't touched since middle school. There's an unfinished collection of about twenty license plates from different states decorating a wall that also features a poster of Don Mattingly lining a base-hit. Since Davey's dad is dead, his mom tells us what to do. She's purposeful and driven. Nobody slacks off and, afterward, she buys us sodas and burgers from McDonald's.

The thing only I know about Davey's basement is that there's a double ceiling. Davey's dad built it when he was still alive. He died when Davey was twelve. He was forty and it was an unexpected heart attack. No previous problems and he was in good shape, golfed all the time, worked on the house when he could, so it was a messed-up situation. Davey heard one grunt while his father was sitting in the living room reading the newspaper in a big chair, and that was it. Dude stopped breathing. A fucked-up shock like that. The summer before, he'd covered the exposed pipes around the perimeter of the basement with a layer of sheetrock, and now the ceiling looks like an upside-down kiddie pool without any water in it. In front of the wall where the Mattingly poster and license plates are tacked, there's a line of halfway hammered-in nails jutting from the sheetrock, each nail spaced about eight inches from the next.

The secret aspect is that I'm the only one who knows Davey put those nails there. He found an old practice net his father used to set up in the backyard to hit golf balls into, and he banged in the nails and hung the net from the sheetrock. Now he smacks baseballs into it. Every night. A thousand swings with the lucky bat he won in a raffle at the team banquet. He's got an adjustable tee he stole from the equipment trailer at school and he sets it up so he can swing at two hundred pitches down and in, two hundred up and in, two hundred belt high over the middle, two hundred up and out, two hundred knee-high on the corner.

I only know about the net and the tee because one night after a game when he went oh-for-five, Davey felt his hands were too slow on pitches high and tight, like they were dragging through the zone. He called me up and told me to come over and I went because Davey never invites people to his house. When I got there, he made me sit on a milk crate and soft-toss balls to him so he could smash them into the net. Over and over. Bang bang bang. Chin high, he said. Put the ball right here toward my neck. I thought we'd do it for ten minutes. We didn't. We did it for an hour-and-a-half. Toss him the ball – smack. Toss him the ball – smack. I was so numbed I felt like I was in Social Studies listening to Mr. Patterson talk about immigration quotas during the Industrial Revolution. Just a few more, Davey kept saying, tears streaming down his face, hands blistered and bleeding as he ripped one toss after another into the net. Gotta get it quicker, damn it. Just a few more. Gotta get quicker.

Neither the net nor the tee is present the day we help deal with the flood. Just the nails in a jagged line sticking from the sheetrock. I'm betting Davey hid the rest of the stuff in his bedroom. I don't know why he doesn't tell anyone how hard he works on his swing. He practices all year long. Winter too. It's how he keeps his weight down for wrestling. A thousand swings makes me lose three-quarters of a pound, he told me. Makes my grip stronger too.

You absolutely do not want Davey clamping on your wrist. His fingers will squeeze your bones like pliers.

Davey's like Archie who can't decide which girl he likes better, Betty or Veronica. With Davey, the question is baseball or wrestling, which one merits top priority. Even though he's baseball captain, I'm betting it'll be wrestling. Davey likes to control shit and baseball has too many variables. You can smack the blood out of a ball and some fucker on the other team can still dive and catch it. Wrestling's more elemental, a one-on-one battle. Two bodies push against each other, flesh on flesh. One body folds.

Davey doesn't like folding.

Maybe it's because it's too sad to chill there with his dad gone, but nobody ever hangs out at Davey's house, except occasional girls. The rest of us pretty much only stop by his front porch. Pick him up and bring him wherever we're going, like Mike D's or Johnny's. There was a rumor once about Davey and Maria Louisa. That's bullshit, Davey said, a rumor only. But I had a feeling it was true.

Stacey's: Girl had a basement bigger than my house. Like twelve rooms and a bathroom she called a changing room. People used it to get out of their bathing suits after swimming in the pool in her backyard. Her yard was surrounded with a wrought-iron fence with metal spikes and we'd never pool-hopped there because nobody wanted to risk his family jewels climbing over it. Swimming with her at night felt like pool-hopping though, like it was a scam to use the luxury pool because Stacey was overweight and her nose was too skinny, sharp like a broken bottle. I dove into the deep end and glided under the surface in the manner of a sleek penguin and when I came up she made jokes that were provocative and there was no reason anyone had to know about it, so we ended up kissing in the hot-tub portion of the pool. Her tongue was surprisingly soft and skilled, and she turned on an underwater red light so the episode glowed like a diabolical porno movie.

Her parents were home but never ventured downstairs and we continued to kiss in the changing room. Her breasts were large and plump and popped out of her swimsuit like two fat grocery-store muffins. Nobody ever had a problem with Stacey's breasts. We migrated into the TV room and inserted a movie in the VCR, a comedy with Richard Pryor. It was funny, but laughter wasn't what we were thinking about. The air conditioning was freezing but its hum was atmospheric and the blanket we huddled beneath was a down comforter that weighed eight hundred pounds and covered us like a promise that was not broken. Afterward, she baked chocolate chip cookies in the basement kitchen while I flipped through a picture book about tragedies that had befallen the original cast members of *Saturday Night Live*. The kitchen had linoleum tiles in a pattern of blue and yellow flowers. The cookies tasted buttery, better than anything my mom or my grandmother ever fed me.

Mike D's: Twice a month on Friday nights, we covered the bumper pool table and played cards. The Yankees were still green on television. Our game was seven-card stud, deuces wild, but sometimes we played anaconda – deal seven cards, keep four, pass two to the left, one to the right, start betting. Five-of-a-kind beat a royal flush. Quarter ante and no buy-in. Beer if we could get it. Potato chips, original flavor or barbecue.

We never invited G-Lover when we played cards. Probably we thought he didn't have any money. Johnny bet high and bluffed and tended to lose big early. Ended up watching green baseball games from the vinyl couch with Mike's little brother Christopher.

Davey accused Lennie of cheating every week. Two wrestlers who liked to beat the shit out of each other. You're a scumbag, Lennie would say, and Mike D. would cut it off right there. Go out to the yard, he'd say, make each other eat grass.

They would and we'd follow. Normally it didn't get bloody. Christopher and Johnny liked to speculate, made bets neither had intentions of paying off. Lennie had more moves and was a better athlete, bigger too. Davey was more vicious. Would bite your wrist if he had to, or squeeze somebody's nuts to win. It was uncomfortable watching them fight outside where the only place to sit was on a rock wall near the forsythia bush Claudia had urinated on three years earlier, back when we were still kids.

There was an old C.B. radio in the basement. If there were no baseball game on TV, Johnny and Christopher liked to monitor the truckers discussing the location of speed traps and the best prostitutes. Once, in the yard, Davey elbowed Lennie in the side of his face and his ear started to bleed, then wouldn't stop, leaking like a hose someone poked a hole in.

Mike's parents weren't home and nobody had a car. I held Lennie's head against my sweatshirt to try and sop the blood. Davey cursed and kicked the rock wall. Inside, the Yanks rallied from three runs down and Johnny said into the radio, Breaker one-nine, breaker one-nine, can anyone take us to the emergency room?

THE NAKED GUY IS DEAD

Sylvia's impatience is a hot orange shimmer. She's drumming her fingers against her teacup and she'd punch me in the face right now if she could, nail me right here in Toledo, in this god-awful antiseptic waiting room, scrubbed up in our prettiest clothes while Josh, our twelve-year-old son, is getting interviewed by the good doctors Weiss and Sutter. The doctors get to decide if Josh is an acceptable candidate for rehab. If they say, no, sorry, your son's a lost cause, we'll have to find another program, but this one in Toledo – Maple Ridge, with the lake and the ice-skating and the organic food – is supposed to be the best. Sylvia's nervous. She wants Josh here, only an hour from home. If Maple Ridge doesn't accept him, and if we can't find somewhere else, Josh goes to juvenile detention.

That's what happens, the judge told us, his face a rusty anvil, when your son is arrested for selling Ecstasy at his middle school.

Sylvia hates me for lots of reasons, but right now it's mostly because I'm reading. We're sitting in these unforgiving plastic chairs that smell like old milk and the good doctors are grilling Josh and he might go to jail. Our twelve-year-old son's a drug dealer and I'm pissing Sylvia off because I'm somehow not zoned out and stunned into paralysis. I'm reading *The New York Times Sunday Magazine,* the year-end issue about all the famous people who died over the past twelve months, and Sylvia's fed up because, really, how can I behave like this, as if life just goes on, as if we haven't irrevocably screwed up our son by failing to raise him with the proper aversion to addicting his pre-teen friends to narcotics?

Leaving aside for a moment the hypocrisy that Sylvia, despite the trauma, despite the stress and the this-can't-be-happenings and the oh-my-Gods – leaving aside that Sylvia remembered to pack in her purse the special Raku green tea bags or whatever she's addicted to drinking like she's a registered and certificated Buddhist monk – leaving beside all that, who the hell is she to judge how I respond to a crisis?

It's not that I'm emotionless. I just don't want to panic. I want Josh to believe I'm here for him. Panicking, finger-drumming on the teacup and all that attendant hostility, that will only freak him out more. Still, all I could think about the whole way here with him in the backseat, asleep or pretending to be, his long greasy hair tilted against the window and covering his eyes, is what did I ever teach this kid? In his twelve years on this planet, what wisdom did I, his father, impart to him?

I could think of only one thing. When he was younger, four or five maybe, before he got skinny and acne and started wearing the black t-shirts, I'd take him to Michigan basketball games. I remember the time-outs, usually toward the end of the game when the idea was to hype the crowd to encourage the Wolverines to go on one final run, and they'd boom the Village People's *YMCA* through the PA. This is the one thing his father taught his son, how to make his hands first into the "Y" spread out above his head, then to curl them into his shoulders to approximate the "M," then the curved "C" to the right side, then above the head again, palms meeting to form the "A." To spell YMCA with his hands – this is what I taught him. He'd practice it at home and we'd head to the arena pretty much just to anticipate the late-game time-outs.

"Read this," I say to Sylvia, handing her the magazine, which entails approximately the same risk as presenting her with a pistol and suggesting she shoot me with it. She rolls her eyes as she often does, basically growls, and returns to the process of rapping her fingers against her tea. "No, really," I urge, but gently. "For real. Just read it."

Since it's the first time in four days I've spoken to her without irritation in my voice, she heaves an enormous disgusted sigh and decides to glance at the story. "The Naked Guy," she says, then starts to read.

Sylvia's a beautiful woman, if a bit less so than when I first met her, cheeks more hollowed now, neck still elegant but beginning to hint at places where skin will eventually flap. When she reads though, she's stunning, her face a portrait of deep devotion, as if the words on the page were written expressly for her. Maybe she knows this, how stunning she looks, the mid-morning light from the lone waiting-room window bronzing her. She reads and her hand brushes her teacup, teasing it with her fingers as if she's petting a dog.

It's not a long article and Sylvia reads quickly, much faster than I do, so it's less than two minutes before the spell of my watching her is broken by her sharp intake of breath. She's reached the part where The Naked Guy – Andrew Martinez, the article says – suffocates himself in a jail cell with a plastic bag. "Damn," she says. "Whoa."

I'd like her to stop holding the teacup at this point and to reach for my hand, but we haven't touched each other in weeks so I don't expect it, and it doesn't happen. When she finishes the article a few seconds later, she hands the magazine back to me. "I didn't know about the rocks thing," she says. "Did you ever see that, what the article says about the rocks? I never saw piles of rocks anywhere."

"No," I say. "I didn't either. I don't remember anything that happened to him after he got kicked out. I didn't even know his real name."

"I did," Sylvia says. "Andrew. I remember that."

For a moment, I'm jealous, as if Sylvia had something going with him back then, but the feeling passes quickly. It was a long time ago when The Naked Guy was famous, when the fuzzed-out pictures of him wearing just a backpack as he walked to class were regular features on the national news, and now, right now, our son's getting interviewed to see whether he's beyond redemption. I drum my fingers, quietly, exaggerated and in slow-motion, against the plastic chair, and pray that in addition to the YMCA gestures, that at some point I taught Josh to sit up straight, to make eye contact from beneath that greasy mat.

Sylvia and I both knew The Naked Guy. Or, at least, we saw him a lot. We were students at Berkeley in the early nineties and met in a class that The Naked Guy was in too. It's true what the article says, he was very polite about his nakedness. He used to spread a sweatshirt out – a red hooded one that said Lifeguard – on the seat in the lecture hall before he sat down. That's what grossed Sylvia out the most about him, the sweatshirt.

"He better wash that thing, like, every day," she wrote to me once in a note during a lecture. "Which thing are you talking about?" I wrote back, even though I knew what she meant. She laughed and almost spit out her gum and the professor glanced up at us from his lectern and Sylvia's cheeks turned red too. I wanted to kiss her right then, and did later that night, for the first time, after we went out for Indian food. "Spicy," she said, one hand patting the collar of my shirt.

The class was a strange one, the professor trying hard to be odd, but actually winding up fairly standard-copy for that campus. A couple hundred people were in the class, including The Naked Guy. It was called "Man and His Legs: A History of the Evolution of Military Transportation," and it was definitely one of those only-at-Berkeley classes, propagated on the idea that the less we as a species had to use our legs in military combat, the more capable we became of killing each other in mass numbers. The hippie professor clearly floated the agenda that we should all surrender our material possessions and spend our days strolling Thoreau-style through the woods. Then we wouldn't be able to sit on chairs in the cold caverns of nuclear submarines and launch missiles with the press of a button that could vaporize thousands of people instantly, our own legs inert beneath gun-metal desks.

"Think about that," the professor repeated about a billion times. "Here is Man stationary. He no longer has to use his legs to run from his enemy because he's far enough away that his enemy cannot strike him. He just sits there and kills. He could be *legless* and still cause massive destruction."

I thought the guy was naïve. Sylvia mostly was steamed he kept saying "man" all the time. "What about women?" she'd say to me, sometimes with a wink if she were in a spicy mood. "Don't we have legs too?"

"Thank God you do," I'd say back. We both loved the irony of a class called Man and His Legs that featured an actual man-student who attended class with his long, bare legs – the whole vast landscape of them, from hip-bone to toes – angling out from his seat. You'd have thought the professor would have appreciated The Naked Guy, how he was a living, breathing example of someone rejecting materialism, but he seemed nearly as irritated with him as he was with Sylvia's laugh. When The Naked Guy raised his hand to comment or ask a question – which was surprisingly often – the professor would cut him off after barely a few words. "Yes, yes," he'd say. "But, no, no, you don't have it quite right."

"He's rude," Sylvia wrote. "The Guy's already naked. Does he have to be humiliated too?"

I thought it was probably the professor who felt humiliated. He'd probably never signed on to have a guy with no clothes ask him questions. Sylvia said he was just jealous, that The Naked Guy was practicing what he only had the guts to preach. "Hypocrite!" she wrote another time.

It could have been, though, that the professor was irritated because The Naked Guy always spent the first ten minutes of each lecture eating. Nothing particularly wrong with someone chowing down in class, but the guy was nude. We tried to be nonchalant about it, but we couldn't help but be fascinated by everything he did. Half the class would watch him eat. He had a wide mouth and huge bright teeth, and the event was a complicated process. In the same careful way he'd spread his sweatshirt on his seat before sitting down, he'd retrieve a paper bag from his backpack and unpack his lunch. It felt like elementary school, the same thing every day, an apple, a carton of milk, and what looked like a homemade peanut butter and jelly sandwich. He'd eat them in the same order too, as if he were superstitious about it – half the apple first, then the sandwich, then the milk, then the rest of the apple.

"I bet he can't buy food anywhere," Sylvia wrote. "It's one thing to go to class naked, but a restaurant can just kick you out. A restaurant can just say, hey, we don't want any naked people in here."

"Health hazard probably," I wrote back.

"I bet he'd like a burrito," she said. "Can you imagine going to school in Berkeley and not being able to buy a burrito?"

I tried and grew immediately, intensely sad. There were four burrito shops on every block in Berkeley, all of them delicious. Not being able to go into any of them felt something like not being able to date any of the beautiful women on campus. That too was a matter of much speculation. If The Naked Guy did date anyone, it wasn't another Berkeley student. He was an attractive dude but, face it, who'd want to be seen giving a goodbye kiss to a naked person on the quad before class? What if the kiss grew passionate and something started to twitch?

The guy was basically an ambulatory statue – a conversation piece, not a person.

"Let's buy him a burrito," I wrote. "Let's get here early one day and drop it off for him." We knew he'd be sitting in the same place. Once The Naked Guy staked out a seat in a lecture hall, it was his for the rest of the semester. Sweatshirt or not.

The next day Sylvia and I met for lunch at El Guapo, and, after we finished eating, returned to the counter to order a burrito to go. "What kind should we get?" I asked.

"Grilled veggie," Sylvia said. "Guy won't wear clothes because he thinks it's immoral. He's gotta be a vegetarian."

"All right," I said, then waved her money away and paid for The Naked Guy's burrito as if I were some kind of gallant knight. We left it for him on his seat with a note that read, "This one's for you, Naked Guy. It's a veggie burrito. Thought you might like it. From Greg and Sylvia in the back."

We were giddy when he walked in and placed his backpack on the floor, then went to spread the sweatshirt. He seemed to pause for a moment as if he didn't know what to make of the package on his seat, as if he wondered if maybe someone else had decided to sit there, but then he saw the note and read it. Next he picked up the burrito and examined it, squeezing it tenderly in his big hands. His expression was skeptical, as if he feared someone were playing a joke on him and, for a moment, we worried he wouldn't eat it. But then he unwrapped it from its foil, sniffed it, and bit into one end. We watched him chew. It didn't seem to matter that he was breaking his tradition of eating the contents of his homemade lunch in a particular order. He gobbled the thing in about five bites, wiped a glop of sour cream from his chin, and turned around with an enormous little kid smile and proffered a thumbs-up to the back row. "Good call on the veggie," I wrote to Sylvia. "Looks like you made The Naked Guy happy."

"I have some experience with that," she wrote. "Making naked guys happy."

I could hardly disagree, not then or later, after we made love in her apartment that night before watching *David Letterman*. It was probably the greatest moment in my life so far when she grinned at me and whispered, "You're a better naked guy."

We graduated in the spring and got engaged shortly thereafter. I asked Sylvia while we were hiking through the Tule Elk Reserve in Point Reyes. She was hungry and wondered if I would pass her some trail mix from my knapsack. "Only if you marry me," I said.

Is there a more glorious sight than the woman you adore, her long legs tanned and sweating, standing at the golden crest of a California hillside, looking down at a grazing herd of prodigiously antlered and endangered deer, ceremoniously spraying an entire bag of trail mix to the wind as if she's spreading the ashes of a deceased loved one?

"It's eleven miles back to the car and that's the only food we had," I said.

"Still want to marry me?" she said.

"More than eating."

By the time The Naked Guy got kicked out of school, we were in San Jose and I'd begun working for Neil, another classmate who'd started Org.com, a company that developed software for on-line calendars and address books. Maybe it was then things began to fall apart for us.

We read about the university's ruling in the Mercury News. Sylvia was furious. "We should do something," she said. "It's not fair. The Naked Guy never bothered anyone."

"He bothered that professor."

"That guy was a prick. We need to do something."

"What?" I said. "What can we do?"

"Protest. Be naked all day. Write a letter to the editor. Something."

"Can we be naked later? I have to go to work."

This is how it happens. Your wife suggests being naked and you decide to go to the office. You go back to Berkeley sometimes for football games or to buy used records or to get high and you never notice piles of rocks in the streets that The Naked Guy built to stop traffic and to arm himself because he thought the CIA was after him. Pretty soon you're following Neil to Michigan because he says, look, everyone else is already in the Bay, there's no one doing this in the Rust Belt, and you think maybe he's right, and then here you are living in Canton and no one knows how to make a decent burrito and you never did anything, never even wrote a letter.

You've never cheated either, but lately you've begun to think about it.

There's a new woman at the office. She's eager and admires you. She's fleshier than Sylvia, more bountiful. She drinks coffee, not tea: tall sugared drinks with clouds of whipped cream. She holds them chest-high and asks you about your family. Your average Midwestern tribe, you tell her. Pretty wife. Smart kid. Nothing special.

Josh had a sophisticated system. If he had pills to sell, he'd wear his book bag slung over his left shoulder. Kids would know to meet him in the library during lunch. He hung out in the paperback area, in a corner hidden by a rotating kiosk of S.E. Hinton novels. He only got caught because it was middle school. Sold two tabs to a boy who went mentally airborne and broke up with his girlfriend in the cafeteria, in front of her friends. The girl was humiliated and, to get back at the boy, told the principal he was stoned. The kid ratted Josh out so he wouldn't get expelled.

I was annoyed when my secretary pulled me from the meeting. More pissed when she said Sylvia was on the phone, urgent. What the hell could be wrong now? But then Silvia was saying something about Josh and drugs, and when she told me we had to go to the police station, I thought she was delusional. When she began to cry, a loud rasp in my ear, I told her the whole thing was her fault. "Too damn permissive," I barked.

"How would you know?" she yelled back. "You're never home. You don't even know him."

It's true. Before we searched Josh's bedroom and found pills and about a dozen bags of marijuana, I hadn't been in there for maybe two years. We have a big house. It's down the block from Neil's and not as big as his, but almost, and we have the same architect. Org.com donates ten percent of its profits to Green

Tech research and both our back porches are built with recycled timber. We live at the end of a cul-de-sac. Our yard rolls down a steep hill and from our back bedroom it looks like we can see forever. Sunsets are majestic. For two years, I returned home after work and sat at my retro gun-metal desk in the study, my own long legs inert, and I didn't set foot in my son's room once.

It almost seems too easy. Find a program, drop off your son, read in the waiting room, shake the doctors' hands, go home. Maybe I wanted it to be harder. Maybe I wanted us to struggle for a while, maybe two weeks of missing work, of driving all over the damn place looking for answers, lost, unhappy, sick from fried road food. Lots of mud and gas stations and blurred vision and something that feels like an epiphany.

But maybe the ride home is miserable enough. The empty back seat kills me. I feel like we took our cat to the shelter where they put animals to sleep and we're returning home without his body. Like we cowered from the job and let the minimum-wage high school kid cremate him while we sat in the waiting room. Sylvia, her hair over her eyes, head leaned against the window, looks like Josh. I reach for her hand as we pull into our driveway. She ignores me.

It's dark now.

Since we've been home, I've sat at the gun-metal desk. No sounds have left my mouth. Fingers numb, eyes glazed, I force myself to heave my legs from the chair and stumble upstairs. Each step is an absurd task, my feet like giant balloons filled with lead. I stagger into the bedroom, but I can't get into bed. Sleeping near my wife seems like lying next to a glacier. She comes out of the bathroom and pulls back the covers. She's holding a book but doesn't open it. For a long time, she looks at me.

I'm pathetic, a dead discolored monument. If the house fell down around me, I'd still be here, rooted, birds and rodents shitting on my shoulders. The hinges of my jaw feel like chains holding a ten-ton drawbridge that hasn't opened for centuries. I can hardly push words out, but I want badly, so badly, to talk.

"The Naked Guy is dead," I say.

Sylvia keeps looking at me for another minute before her eyes soften. I think maybe there's some kind of opening. My fingers feel as if they've turned to stone, but I force them to move. I unbuckle my belt. It's an effort because I've gotten so flabby, and because my fingers are thick rocks, but somehow I manage to wriggle out of my jeans and boxers, to pull off my shirt.

My wife doesn't look away, doesn't turn to her book. At last, she swings her feet off the bed, walks toward me slowly and begins to unbutton her top. Then she steps out of her pants and underwear. We turn to the window. We don't hold hands – there's still a distance between us, that whole sonless drive back from Ohio – but we're naked now.

We stand in the cold and shiver, looking west.

ACKNOWLEDGEMENTS

Many thanks to Steve Gillis and Dan Wickett for believing in these stories and to Matt Bell for making them sing (or grunt, or whatever it is they do). Much gratitude as well to David Marshall Chan, Lewis Robinson, Lesléa Newman, Alan Davis, Mike White, Baron Wormser, Richard Hoffman, Joan Connor, Scott Beal, Karen Smyte and Sarah Andrew-Vaughn for helping me along the way and to Junot Diaz, Julie Orringer, Adam Mansbach, Steve Amick, Davy Rothbart and Laura Kasischke for showing me how to do the thing right. Constant inspiration comes from Roger Bonair-Agard, Patricia Smith, Kevin Coval, Patrick Rosal, Aracelis Girmay, Regie Gibson, Ross Gay, Tim Seibles, Ben Cohen, Jon Sands and Jeff McDaniel and, of course, all the students who bring dazzle to their own pages including, but not limited to: Angel Nafis, Maggie and Coert Ambrosino, Caronae Howell, Big Ben Alfaro, Adam Falkner, Molly Raynor, Lauren Whitehead, Gahl and Jon Liberzon, Mike and Chris Moriarty, Mike Kulick, Daniel Bigham, Aimée Le, Fiona Chamness, Paco, Matt Dagher-Margosian, Maggie Hanks, Erin Murphy, Courtney Whitler, Arhm Choi, Erica Rosbe, Claire Forster, Carlina Duan, Emma Hamstra, Emily Berry, Sara Ryan, Glenna Benitez, Anthony Zick, Kate Rogow, Beth Johnson and Allison Kennedy.

Thanks also to invaluable friends and supporters: Pamela Waxman, Lisa Dengiz, Julie Cohen, JR, David Saxen and Nancy Puttkamer, Nancy and Drake Ambrosino, Kathy and David Falkner, Ken and Laura Raynor, Nina and Gary Rogow, Lori Roddy, John Weiss, Milt Liu, Michael Kim, Joe Eagleeye, Marty Shaffer, Brad Harris, Doug Petraco, Keith Goggin, Tracy Rosewarne, Ellen Stone and the Pi-Hi English Department.

Big ups to Andy, Jimmy and Laura for growing up in the same circumstances, to Joan and Steve Kass for raising us and to Julius and Sam for willing to be raised.